About Donna Maree Hanson

Donna Maree Hanson is a traditionally and independently published author of fantasy, science fiction and horror. She also writes paranormal romance under the pseudonym of Dani Kristoff. Her dark fantasy series (which some reviewers have called 'grim dark'), Dragon Wine, was published by Momentum Books (Pan Macmillan digital imprint). Book 1: *Shatterwing* and Book 2: *Skywatcher* are out now in digital and print on demand. In April 2015, she was awarded the A. Bertram Chandler Award for 'Outstanding Achievement in Australian Science Fiction' for her work in running science fiction conventions, publishing and broader SF community contribution. Donna also writes young adult science fiction, with *Rayessa and the Space Pirates* and *Rae and Essa's Space Adventures* out with Escape Publishing. In 2016, Donna commenced her PhD candidature researching feminism in *popular romance at the University of Canberra. Her first Indie book, Argenterra*, was published in late April 2016. *Argenterra* is the first in an epic fantasy series (the Silverlands) suitable for adult and young adult readers. *Oathbound*, Book Two and *Ungiven Land*, Book Three were published in 2017. Donna lives in Canberra with her partner and fellow writer Matthew Farrer.

Sign up to Donna's newsletter for special offers and new publication news.
http://donnamareehanson.com

Also by Donna Maree Hanson

Love and Space Pirates Series (Science fiction romance)

Rayessa and the Space Pirates (Escape Publishing)

Rae and Essa Space Adventures (Escape Publishing)

Opi Battles the Space Pirates

The Silverlands (Epic fantasy)

Argenterra, The Silverlands Book One

Oathbound, The Silverlands Book Two

Ungiven Land, The Silverlands Book Three

Dragon Wine Series (Dark Fantasy)

Shatterwing, Dragon Wine Part One

Skywatcher, Dragon Wine Part Two

Deathwings, Dragon Wine Part Three

Bloodstorm, Dragon Wine Part Four (due 2017)

Opi Battles the

Space Pirates

By
Donna Maree Hanson

Copyright information

Title: Opi Battles the Space Pirates

Author: Donna Maree Hanson

ISBN 978-0-9757217-5-9 —ebook

ISBN 978-0-9757217-6-6 —print

Copyright © by Donna Maree Hanson 2017

National Library of Australia Cataloguing-in-Publication entry : (ebook)

Creator: Hanson, Donna Maree, author.

Title: Opi battles the space pirates / Donna Maree Hanson.

ISBN: 9780975721759 (ebook)

Series: Hanson, Donna Maree. Love and space pirates.

Subjects: Science fiction.

Romance fiction.

Space pirates.

To Nicole Murphy who teaches me about love everyday

Chapter One

Explosive Personality

Opeia Gayens was having a bad day. She was tired, oh so tired, and a wee bit cranky. Running AllEarth Corp had its highs and its lows. So far today had been one of the lows. And it wasn't getting any better. Not only had her daughter, Rae, just told her that she didn't want to join the company or want her inheritance, this executive interview with Jors Finksy had taken a bad turn.

Finksy held out a hot pink, round object about the size of a tennis ball that looked suspiciously like a plastic explosive. 'This is a bomb,' he declared, waving at her. 'I'm going to take you with me.'

Opeia let out a sigh, moved her knee to key her distress alarm. 'That,' she said, 'is rather counter-productive.'

It had been a run-of-the-mill ethics appraisal. Obviously, the testing regime designed to filter out space pirates, or those likely to be suborned by space pirates, was more stressful than she anticipated for her employee to take such drastic measures.

Jors had standing-on-end, spikey, white hair and his red, sweating face sported puffy cheeks and very pale eyes. His burnished-silver body suit hugged his plump frame in a less than complimentary manner. Not the sort to bring a bomb to a meeting.

Her security chief, Mueller, was going to get an earful for his team letting this incendiary device through the screening procedures. It signalled a lapse that wasn't acceptable. She eyed the bomb. It had no discernible controls or wires or lights. It looked like a lurid, ball of soft, mouldable plastic that a child might play with.

Finksy stood up suddenly, waving the ball around. Instinctively, Opeia leant back. Where was her security team anyhow?

'You were going to dismiss me from my job. It's all I have...'

Opeia blinked. She hadn't been about to sack the poor fellow, but that outcome seemed inevitable now.

Distracted by security taking their time, Opeia was taken by surprise when Finksy thrust the bomb into her face. Instinctively, she slapped his hand and the bomb flew up. She leapt for it in case it would explode on impact. She caught it with one hand and with the other, punched her terrorist under the chin. The man wasn't expecting it and went down.

Letting out a breath, she had one second of relaxation and then she noticed the bomb started to sweat in her hand and was slightly warm. Leaning down, she said into her intercom, 'Polly, where the hell is security!'

'Oh? We thought you'd triggered it by accident.'

'I have a bomb in my hand and an unconscious executive who will come around very soon. Get the team in here now.'

Polly didn't answer but in about thirty seconds her door slid open. 'Don't move,' the lead security guy said. 'Smithy, get up here with the analyser.'

Opeia swallowed and looked slowly down at her hand. 'Geez.' Bubbles appeared on surface of the ball. There was a chemical reaction going on. The hot pink bomb was definitely giving off heat. Why had she tackled for the bomb anyhow? Was she insane?

Smithy, face covered in a shock proof shield, aimed the pointy end of the analyser at her. 'Plastic explosive. DNA key.'

'Can't you get a bin or something? I don't want it going off in my hand.'

Smithy backed up, head titled on the side. 'Containment possible,' he spoke into the mic.

A rumble from the back of the door and a trolley came in, bearing a two metre by two metre metal box.

Smithy keyed a small panel. 'Now, Ma'am, a drawer will slide out. Quickly place the device onto it and back away. It will shut rapidly and should contain the blast.'

Opeia looked up. 'Should? Great.'

From the bottom end of the metal box, a square door opened up. It could hold a basket ball-sized object. With lips compressed, Opeia bent her knees, bringing the bomb closer. The bubbles on the surface of the bomb resembled boils now. The heat it gave off was starting to burn her palm. Carefully, she placed her hand near the bottom of the box and started tilting her hand to allow the ball to slide off.

Finksy sat up suddenly and shook his head. 'Stop!' he said. Opeia jerked her hand with surprise. The bomb dropped. She snatched her hand back. A security guard charged forward tackling her to the ground to shelter her with his body. The drawer shut with a snap. The containment box jumped and a loud boom sounded from inside. From where the little drawer had retracted, the metal had melted and fumes were rising.

The guard levered himself off her. 'Pardon me, Ma'am.' The label on his hazard gear gave his name as Muri. He offered his hand and assisted her to stand.

'Thank you, Mr Muri.'

Another security man came up and sprayed her hands. The burning stopped as the spray cooled her skin.

Two burly ones grabbed Finksy. They brought him in front of her.

Her hands were red and the skin had started to peel. Compared to what could have happened. No hands. Or no body. She had come off lightly. 'Mr Finksy. I am sorry to have to tell you but you're fired…and under arrest.'

The containment box was wheeled out. The security team followed, along with Finksy who was quite verbal in his resentment. When they left, Polly buzzed. 'Chief Mueller for you.'

'Send him in.'

'He's not actually here, sorry. On comms.'

Too chicken to face her. Damn the man. Walking to her desk, she keyed her comms. 'Mueller what the actual?' she yelled at him. He opened his mouth and kept it open. 'Nobody responded to my distress alarm and how did that goddam bomb get through screening?'

'Ms Gayens…Opeia…'

'Don't try to sweet talk me.' Mueller's bull dog face loomed on the viewscreen.

'I won't. The bomb was a new type of material,' he rushed on before she could interrupt again. 'We had rumours of it being in production but our screening wasn't calibrated. It is now.' He let out a breath. 'The non-response is a bit more difficult to explain.' He ran his fingers through his short cropped hair. 'It had been reported to me that you accidentally set off your distress alarm seven times in the last month. My men advise that you were pretty pissy at them for the repeated interruptions when they responded as per procedure.'

Opeia nodded, recollecting the mayhem. The distress switch had been relocated to under the desk so she could call for help without anyone knowing, unfortunately she kept bumping it. Her annoyance at having important and confidential meetings and video conferences interrupted had been quite strong and verbal. May have involved threats too. She chewed the inside of her cheek. 'Put the location of my distress alarm back on our regular agenda. I don't want to be left vulnerable like that again.'

'I'll tighten security measures.'

'No! Goddam it Mueller! They are so tight already.' As it was she hardly saw normal people. Her children were exempt from the security procedures but not anyone else. At times it was a tad embarrassing. *I hope the cavity search wasn't too uncomfortable, Mr...*

'But not tight enough. Today is a good example.'

'You've explained today. It won't happen again.' He opened his mouth to protest but she raised her hand. 'Your hand to hand training came in useful.' She thought this would divert him.

He growled. 'Ms Gayens you aren't meant to tackle people with bombs or grab the devices yourself. May I remind you that you could have died if it had been another type of bomb?'

'I know. I'm sorry. I just reacted when he thrust the bomb in my face and no one had come to help."

He let out a sigh and rubbed his hand through his hair. 'I see.'

Opeia thought she could wrap this up with another diversion. 'Say, can you send me an update on that bomb material. DNA triggered you say? Let me get across that.'

'Very well. Done and agreed. The information will be sent to you by the end of the day. My advice is that you should not have ill effects from holding the bomb except for some superficial burns.'

She held up her hands. 'I got that part.'

'Although I wish you hadn't tackled the man and taken it.

'I know. I don't know what came over me. Spur of the moment—panic. It was entirely stupid. It won't happen again.'

Mueller grunted and she keyed off. Turning to her handheld, she entered in the information about Finksy's dismissal and sent a memo to her personnel manager to start new recruitment activity. Then she slumped across her desk. She was sick to the bone of this. Over it. That's why Rae's message had gutted her. If she wasn't doing this for her daughter why was she doing it? Essa, her other daughter, had already bailed a year ago.

Sometime later her office door chimed. 'May I come in?' Polly, her personal assistant, asked as she poked her head through the gap in the sliding door. Polly was a few years younger than Opeia and had such an easy going personality that Opeia thought of her as a friend. About five foot five, trim with a pixie-like face, she was a trendy dresser and was forever ribbing Opeia about her penchant for pantsuits for business or shapeless coveralls when travelling on space cruisers. Polly argued they marred her beauty, where Opeia thought they hid a multitude of sins, like a peach shaped butt, well-rounded belly, largish breasts and generous thighs.

'Sure, Pol. What is it?' Opeia sat up and self-consciously tugged at the tunic top of her pale lemon, pantsuit. The material was self-cleaning and wrinkle proof. What could be easier?

Polly raised her eyebrows and pursed her lips, then let out a sigh before continuing. 'I have a priority-keyed message for you from someone called,' she looked down at her handheld. 'Owain McDevitt.'

'Who?'

Polly sighed. 'Owain McDevitt.' She scrolled through the page on her handheld. 'McDevitt Enterprises. You completed the takeover of his transport companies last year. All the official paperwork is completed.'

'Refresh my memory. What did I do to him, actually?'

Chapter Two

Dinner Invitation

Polly checked her handheld again. 'You bought out McDevitt's stake in Spacefreight Expo. Overbid on his takeover bid of Buckley's Bulk Transport Fleet. Gutted the ships in inventory in Spacefreight Expo and Buckley's and on-sold them at a huge profit.'

'I see. And?'

'You left him the planet.'

'Planet?'

'Yes, small agricultural world. Grows potatoes mostly, I think. Islay 2.'

'Why did I do that?'

'My notes say you didn't want to leave him desperate and you had no interest in grubbing in the dirt.'

Opeia smiled. 'I was having a good day then.' Her gaze rested on Polly, who shifted from foot to foot with nervous anxiety. Opeia frowned. 'What does he want? My blood?'

Polly's dark eyes flicked up from the handheld and tugged at her short cropped hair. She shrugged one handed. 'It's marked private. Do you want to see it or shall I zap it straight to trash?'

Opeia keyed up her own handheld. 'Give me a minute. I want to refresh my memory.' She read her takeover notes. It was McDevitt Enterprises who owned the stake in Spacefreight Expo. Asset rich. Low profits. Possible source of pirate activity. It had been a fat fish waiting to be fried. It had been an odd setup. Who structured their business that way? Underutilising assets. The balance sheets were a beacon for any shark who was looking for prey. It was almost too good to be true. Or it was suspect.

As she considered it the latter, she'd wanted the outfit gutted and closed. She scrolled to the next page. She'd left McDevitt a planet. It was small, agricultural and was of limited interest to her. She could have taken it too, but hadn't. Her notes did say that she had to leave the man something. Her notes said: were space pirates interested in potatoes? Her memory stirred. AllEarth Corp invested, divested, took over and reconfigured companies daily. She remembered feeling soft-hearted for McDevitt. He hadn't owned the business long. A new kid on the block and she'd never met the man. Was it because she couldn't find that he was linked to pirates himself? She flicked to the next page. He had a daughter, Lucinda, aged fourteen. His wife had passed away in a terraforming accident five years previously. It was probably the daughter that had made her soft around the edges. A quick scan of the photo reminded her that Lucinda McDevitt looked a bit like her own daughters. Same dark eyes, same brown hair cut into a bob.

Another page flicked over. McDevitt was ex-military. He specialised in security. How did he go from security to owning a number of companies? Was he that good at his job? Or did he come into an inheritance or was he up to something dodgy? Well, if he had been, he wasn't doing it now. She'd taken those transport companies and ended them. He could hardly use his planet to help pirates, except as a base. She checked the coordinates of the planet. It really wasn't central enough to be useful to them. It was in a backwater, barely within reach of the last jumpgate in the sector.

And he had a message for her. Interesting.

She looked up from her handheld. 'Okay. Send it through, Pol. Is Rani still around?'

'No. She is off until we leave tomorrow. Do you want me to call her up?'

'No, it can wait. We'll have time while the ship is in preflight and we will still have comms.'

Rani was Opeia's second executive assistant. Polly looked after the social, but Rani was the numbers gal. She'd worked on the McDevitt takeover bid. Must have done as Rani had some role in all of them. She figured McDevitt wasn't going to challenge her on the numbers as the deal was done and dusted. His signed share transfer was lodged with the galactic registry on Earth. The file in her handheld said the deal was closed. There were no loose ends. So why had he sent her a message?

Polly left the office and went back to her desk. A moment later, her comms unit buzzed.

'Putting the message through now, Ms Gayens.'

'Thanks.'

A smiling face greeted her. It was a prerecorded video message. A bit hard to have a live conversation across space due to the distance and resultant time lag so recorded was the way to go. 'Ms Gayens. Forgive this intrusion on your time. I know it has been some months since our deal was sealed, but I wanted to convey to you my thanks for leaving me Islay 2. It was very kind of you and for some time now I felt...' he shrugged, looked down at his hands clasped on his knees. 'No, needed, to express my gratitude.'

McDevitt looked fortyish. Opeia was tempted to check his stats but decided to do that later. He had dark hair, conventionally cut around the ears and neck, bright blue eyes, the colour of a summer sky, set wide. A round, open face, with cheeks that dimpled when he smiled. He was seated outside, on a balcony or patio. In the background was a mountain range, backlit by a setting sun. A smattering of clouds turned purple and pink in the evening sky. Opeia cocked an eyebrow at the backdrop. It looked real, not a vid display.

On Earth, it wasn't often you got to see a sunset like that, not in the city at least. Islay 2, she supposed, was impressive for a potato farm. It looked rustic but including the planet scene as the backdrop was a nice touch.

She paused the message. Had she been kind? She was uncomfortable with the label. Had she really said to Rani that she didn't want to make him desperate? She hadn't taken him over to enlarge her corporate empire, but to gut the pirates' access to transport ships. Did he even know what was happening in Spacefreight Expo and Buckleys? Did he understand her motives? For sure, she'd made a nice, tidy profit, but in the scale of AllEarth Corp's annual earnings it was a drop in the bucket.

Her attempts to clean up her company had been extensive and expensive: ethics training, internal reviews, doubling of approvals required for financial expenditure, personal interviews with candidates for new executive positions and performance reviews for the existing ones, background checks, including government security clearance processes. It had been exhausting. Nothing seemed to work completely. She'd cut out some rot, but the source of the infection remained.

Her pending trip was to root out more of the rot, draw out the source of the infection. A big gamble. Last time, the space pirates had come close to taking the whole damn thing. She had been tortured, her daughters kidnapped. It had been close. She'd taken steps so it couldn't happen that way again, even if her plans failed this time. She was hoping her plans wouldn't fail.

She checked the time left to play on the message. McDevitt had more to say it seemed. She released the hold button. 'I understand you are heading into this sector shortly. I wonder if it would be possible to meet so I can thank you in person. Dinner at *Hotel Magnifique*? Space station Beta C? My treat.'

He grinned.

She froze the image, heart thudding.

That sounded awfully like he was asking her on a date. Nah, that didn't sound right. Opeia didn't go on dates. Even though now she was a widow, and technically could go on a date, she wouldn't know where to begin. She did business meetings, working coffee breaks and high-powered lunches where deals were made. When she did do the social thing it was still business, cocktail parties, boring, elaborate meals and stuffy functions where a speaker harangued one on whatever topic was topical. All that effort was to further the prospects of AllEarth Corp, not her social life. Besides being too busy, she was rich and that made her a target for all kinds of things: scams, hold ups, black mail, abduction, seduction and death. Her bomb scare just now was just one attempt in a string of many failed ones. Not that she'd had much seduction in her life. Her security team would have kittens if she started going out with random strangers on dates. God forbid if she had a sex life. Her security detail would be examining the condoms to ensure they were sound to protect her from disease and testing the champagne to make sure she wasn't drugged. She laughed and then stopped suddenly. It was too stupid, too awful, too sad but true. Her security would do those invasive things.

Sitting back in her chair, she tapped her finger on the desk. She hadn't been on a date since she had been in her late teens. That had been with her ex-husband, Carl. God forbid she repeated that mistake. These days, she didn't even know what to do on a date. At the thought of it, her palms became all sweaty and she wrung her hands together. It was impossible wasn't it?

Immediately, she replayed the message, trying to play it down. He couldn't be asking her on a date. Her mind was on a broken record. No one asked her on dates. She never met people socially. It was all business. All of it. Government soirees. Business conventions. Board meetings. Those horrible, emotionally bereft meetings stretched to infinity in her mind. No real connection. No unscripted conversations. No free ranging. No touching! Why did the thought of doing something so ordinary as going on a date send her into a panic?

On the fourth run through the message still sounded like he was asking her on a date. There was something in his manner, his smile, the intimacy of a dinner or was that just her response to his message? She was attracted to him? *Oh no!* She started to sweat. That meant personal time. No business. Woman versus man. No shield. Nothing to hide behind. Raw Opeia and a man. Her nails were getting rather short as she gnawed on them. Mind working overtime. How did he even know she was going to that part of space? He'd obviously accessed her flight plan. She'd have to ask Polly if publicity had released it yet. *Cheeky!*

Had she met Owain McDevitt face-to-face previously? She ran his name and image through her personal database where she logged all her personal contacts. Everyone she met was listed there. Useful when you met so many people, sometimes just once. It came up blank.

Considering the idea, she rubbed her chin, and then eased back into her chair. Her stomach rumbled and her handheld chimed. She looked at it. Dinner meeting with the head of AllEarth Corp security, Chief Mueller. How long had she been wallowing here over this invitation? She sent a message asking the security team for an extra ten minutes. Why she needed that long escaped her.

She keyed a short response to McDevitt. At first it said 'No, thanks' and 'Can't possibly'. Then she squinted at the screen and chewed her bottom lip. That's just chicken, she observed. Well, what was she going to do then?

Letting out a pent up breath, she retyped her response. Not quite up to recording a vid message. She didn't have the time or the inclination. The words 'Happy to meet over dinner, Opeia Gayens' glowed on the screen. She hesitated. Her hand hovered over the send key. Was it too short? Should she thank him? No, that was too gushy. Damn it just send the thing. Then she hit the button. The message was gone. Her heart raced so hard she thought she was having a cardiac arrest. She'd just said yes to a date with a complete stranger. It wasn't earth shattering so why was she close to a panic attack? *So stupid!*

He wasn't going to eat her. A giggle escaped her. Not on the first date, at least. Where were these aberrant thoughts coming from? She screwed up her eyes, wondering about her vid movie collection. If her therapist knew where her thoughts tended she'd put her on medication. Opeia shrugged. Maybe she wouldn't. Maybe her therapist would pat her on the back and say good girl. Well, not in so many words.

After a few calming breaths, she coded the date into her personal itinerary and put a reminder in for Polly to lock down the details, such as the local time and date.

As she stood up to freshen up for her next meeting, she cringed. She'd said yes to a dinner date. She baulked at the thought and tried to keep calm about it. She coded the appointment priority so Polly would know not to quash it without checking with her first just in case she ran out of time or had to juggle meetings.

If she had time she was doing the dinner thing with McDevitt. That was one scary meeting. Just thinking of it had her heart stammering. *Get a grip!* All the things that could get in the way of meeting with him loomed large in her mind. It helped calm her down. The date was most likely not going to happen. She was likely to be inundated with business. Business came first. At least, for the time being.

With five minutes to spare, she went to freshen up before her next meeting. It was a short trip to AllEarth Towers through a direct underground tunnel on a mag lev vehicle.

In the company dining room sitting across from Chief Mueller and his two top aides, Fritz and Frantz, Opeia picked at her salad. The salad indicated a good food choice for the weight conscious executive, but did nothing to inspire her in the face of her least favourite meeting. The head of her security team looked serious, glowering at her with his bushy eyebrows sprinkled with grey that bobbed up and down as he spoke. A face that had avoided any rejuvenating treatments, seamed with creases from nose to mouth. Jowls wobbled under his chin. A craggy faced bear, she thought of him. From the intent look in his eye and the length of the agenda, Opeia knew this meeting was going to take ages. Their earlier spat over the DNA coded bomb was forgotten, except for the extra five items added to the agenda. Eyeing her salad, she decided she needed something more, something that would assist her to endure the next hour or so. She scanned the menu and ordered a very big ice cream sundae with extra whipped cream, dense caramel sauce and additional peanut ice cream for dessert. She was going to need the pick me up.

'Ms Gayens,' the security chief continued. 'About this latest change to your itinerary...'

She began to roll her eyes and stopped, realising what change he meant. He knew about her date. *Damn it.* She took in a breath, and toyed with a slice of tomato. It was beneath her to treat her security chief with so little respect so she asked, 'Is there a problem?' in her most calm voice.

'Yes, but not an insurmountable one. Provided you approve these preliminary security measures and abide by these restrictions,' he said handing her a list. 'Then we should be able to allow this McDevitt fellow on board the ship.'

She winced. 'I believe he invited me to dine on Space Station Beta C.'

'Out of the question.'

Opeia lowered her eyes, flicked the plate of salad to the side and dived into the ice cream sundae that had just been delivered to the table. 'Why? I'm going to be on Space Station Beta C anyway.'

'The venue does not allow weapons. Your security team will be disadvantaged.'

Opeia licked cream and caramel topping from her spoon. 'You're not going to station a security team outside the restaurant, are you? I mean station security is acceptable isn't it? Surely you have plans of the station and can work out if there are any vulnerabilities from where our ship is docked to the hotel? I'm already sleeping on ship rather than the station under your recommendations. I'd really like to meet Mr McDevitt. Can't you do a risk assessment or something?'

'We have. I don't like the risk you're taking. What do you know about this man?'

'As much as anyone does, I suppose. I've never met him though. You have some intel that I should know about? I thought he was ex-military and a security specialist before he went potato farming.'

Mueller checked his handheld. 'No, Ma'am. Nothing extra to add. That all checks out. I know nothing more than you do.'

Opeia scanned the list of items to be discussed. They were still stuck on item two. Fatigue was starting to wear her down. The caramel and ice cream was helping but if she didn't finish, she was going to be wiped for their launch the next day. She keyed up another sundae order. She was going to need the sugar and the fat.

'Look. Do some more in-depth work on McDevitt. It is by no means certain I will meet him anyway. Draft up a security plan based on the station's and the restaurant's restrictions. Then you can brief me on the drill beforehand. Okay?'

Mueller nodded. 'Now item three. The flight plan. My team have gone over it and we think that you are going too close to Praght space. There has been some pirate activity there. We suggest you alter the route to go through the Prime Five jumpgate.'

Opeia gave the flight plan a cursory look. 'Fine,' she replied. The navigator would complain tomorrow when she boarded. Let them fight it out.

She was finishing off the second sundae when they had done with the first five items on the list. Chief Mueller ground his teeth. When she protested item six. 'You can't be serious. You want to interrogate McDevitt for three hours and have him undergo a strip search before you will even let him enter the restaurant? No!'

'Ms Gayens. We have your safety to maintain.'

No wonder she didn't date anyone. 'Look, you can do more in-depth searching on his life, his activities. If you find anything nefarious we'll talk again. If you come up with something bad, I won't meet him. But you won't be subjecting my 'date' to those,' she tapped on the agenda item, 'procedures. Understand?'

'Yes,' Mueller replied. 'So one bodyguard and possibly Polly to accompany you to dinner?' He made some notations.

Opeia clenched her jaw. 'Yes. No. Oh I don't know. Check back with me later though. I may change my mind about the whole thing.'

'Change it? But you haven't' decided.'

Opeia let out a big sigh. She was a rich woman after all. She couldn't possibly go alone. Could she? She'd talk to Polly. Polly went on dates. She'd know what the deal was.

Hopefully, McDevitt understood the difficulties she had to go through just to meet for dinner. He wanted to thank her for not wiping the floor with him. That took guts. Besides, she mused, he had a nice smile. She may be an older woman, but she did still have hormones. Fortyish wasn't old these days. Her daughters weren't the only ones who liked good looking men. That started her thinking down a particular path. When was the last time she'd had sex? A very long time ago. She'd been too busy and married to Gayens, who she hadn't touched with a barge pole once she knew what his whole motivation was. Come to think of it, her love life hadn't been that good anyway. Gayens was always thinking about his experiments and hardly noticed his young wife. Once he'd got the funding he required, Opeia had faded into the background.

Was she bitter? Opeia hardly knew. She'd got a daughter out of it, and a cloned daughter. It was something she supposed. Could one forget how to have sex?

Later, as she went to her quarters, she mused about her life while she brushed her hair and got ready for bed. At forty-two, she technically still ovulated. If she wanted to she could start a whole new family, a whole new life. She poked a tongue at her reflection.

If only she wasn't the majority shareholder of AllEarth Corp. She had a duty to the firm. Her family had built the business empire up over the years. People depended on her for their livelihood. Then there was those blasted space pirates. She couldn't rest until she had ripped them screaming out of the bowels of her firm. She shuddered at the memory of being held hostage by Masher and his crew. That had been a painful and dangerous lesson. She wouldn't be caught out like that again. This time she was going to be ready. Her own plans were still unfolding.

Compartmentalised in her system too, plan A through to E. There were many strings in her bow. Not all of them were known to her team. A woman had to keep some things secret.

Too wound up to sleep, she put on an exercise program. Her virtual instructor put her through her paces. After an hour of that, she fell on the bed, her eyes closing after a few breaths. Knackered.

Chapter Three

Take Off

In her suite on her sleek, little cruiser *Holdfast,* Opeia ran down her 'to do' list with a finger, while the ship's crew completed the last of the preparations to break orbit. She ticked off a few items, approved some acquisitions and reviewed some interview records and personnel background checks. Comms chimed. She looked up from her handheld and saw the light blink green. It was a secure transmission. She keyed the receive button. 'Dayton?'

Dayton's dark features filled the viewscreen. His smooth scalp gleamed in the light. 'Ms Gayens. I'm glad I caught you before you left.' He looked down, possibly at his own handheld. His eyes flicked up. 'I'm afraid I don't have your final itinerary. I may need to contact you while you are away.'

'It is probably finding its way to you. Update?'

'I was able to divide up the lots to pass unnoticed by most of the players. However, my activities did catch the eye of a certain senator.'

'Which one?'

'Burr.'

Opeia smiled a small smile. Dayton's dark brown eyes sparkled a little. 'A friend?'

'Some of the time.'

'A confidante?'

She hesitated. It was not easy to trust people, even those in her employ. Her plan called for fractured play—many hands moving at once, none knowing what the other was doing. She was at the centre, controlling the strings, manipulating the tide. One wrong word in this game she was playing could mean someone compromised or dead. 'Let's just say that Senator Burr and I are old fencing partners.'

Dayton nodded and grinned. 'It will take another three weeks to sell the rest of those shares on the open market. In the small packets you require.'

'Institutional investors?'

'Mostly. Some investment funds. Several hundred individual investors.'

She nodded. 'Good. You completed the transfer of the rest?'

'In progress. They are currently being registered in a nominee company until you are ready. I have filed the requisite notifications to the stock exchange for when you give the word.'

'Good, report back when you are done. I may have other work for you. We need to see how this trip plays out and how much longer the sales activity can remain under the radar.'

'The exchange is happy with what you have disclosed to them. But have requested to be notified if the share parcels increase in size or we reach a change in beneficial ownership.'

'Good. See you then.'

'Very well. Safe travels.'

She keyed off and floated over to her coffee station. She took a sip on the straw and sighed. Caffeine. Her faithful friend. It helped with the microgravity-induced nausea too. She hadn't eaten anything since the two ice cream sundaes the night before. She shouldn't have indulged herself. Where was her control?

She keyed up a secure channel. A familiar face appeared on screen: red hair, ginger goatee and dark eyes framing a rather ponderous, freckled nose. Opeia thought the senator was a well-preserved sixty but suspected he was older. 'Senator Burr. How nice to see you.'

The senator leant forward over his desk as if looking behind her. 'Going somewhere I see.'

She glanced behind her, saw that the emergency netting was hanging on the bulkhead. 'Off planet on business.'

'I see. Anything I should know about? AllEarth Corp is a big player you know. These share transactions are making me nervous. If anything is amiss I should know before...well before...'

Opeia studied the older man. She'd known him since the early days and he had been a friend of her parents. He'd comforted her when they had died. Although the official version was accidental death, Senator Burr and she knew, it had been assassination. They hadn't found the culprit. Any hard evidence they had had been compromised. Her bet was on Carl Gayens. Proving it had been too hard. 'Just some reorganising of my portfolio, Senator. Nothing to worry about. I'll keep you informed if there is anything major going on.'

He nodded. 'About that favour you asked me for.'

Her eyebrows lifted in query. 'Can you swing it?'

'It is in train. Send me through the coordinates for each unit. You can send updates to them if you need to change their location. But, be careful.'

'I will. Say hello to Madelyn for me. Please let her know I will try to be at her next fundraiser. Timing is off for this week.'

'She understands. My wife is an old hand at these things. The donation you sent more than made up for your absence. You are too generous. If you keep it up, soon she won't have to run fundraisers, only threaten to and let you know so you can send another donation.'

'Where is the fun in that? You know she likes meeting the celebrities and the politicians and being the centre of the social whirl. The money is only the cream on the cake.'

'Too true. Keep me posted if you need any other favours.'

'I will.'

She'd only just keyed off when her captain hailed her. 'Ms Gayens. We seem to have trouble with the waybill on our cargo.'

'Oh really? Send the query to my comms.'

The waybill came up. Her special cargo was missing an inspection certificate.

'Riley?' she spoke into the comms after calling up another secure channel.

Curly-headed Colonel Riley, who had grey hair at his temples scowled into the viewer. 'Ms Gayens?'

'The waybill on shipment 457 is missing an inspection certificate. I thought you were handling that.'

He scowled further and scanned his handheld. 'There it is. It somehow got separated from the rest of the documentation.' He punched a button. 'Captain Graves should have it now.'

'Thank you. You coming onboard Riley?'

He looked up. 'Of course. My shuttle leaves in five minutes.'

'I won't keep you, then. See you onboard.' Riley was useful muscle. She had hired him after her escape from Masher and his band of pirates. He'd been in the military, off-world forces. He was gruff, but she liked him.

Opeia ended the transmission. The certificate must have gone through because Captain Graves had started the pretest sequences for engine start up. The thrum of the engine vibrated against the soles of her feet. She decided against contacting the captain again, considering if the certificate hadn't passed muster she would have been told fairly promptly. The customs inspectors would have to be leaving for the orbiting station soon.

Opeia opened a secure page on her handheld and ticked off another item on her to do list.

Her door chimed. A blue uniformed, young man hovered there, keeping vertical with his booted feet tucked under the door seal. Tall, dark, well-muscled with regular features, she hadn't seen him before. He had an East Asian appearance.

'Yes?'

'Forgive the intrusion, Ma'am. Colonel Mueller requested I report to you. I am to be your personal bodyguard for this trip.'

'Oh and what am I to call you?'

'Pravi, Ma'am.'

'Nice to meet you, Pravi. I'm sure we'll deal well together. How are things progressing for departure?'

'Well, Ma'am. We are scheduled to leave in two hours and fifteen minutes.'

'Good. Call me Ms Gayens if you please. The Ma'am is a bit...' She shrugged. 'Well it makes me feel old.'

'Very well, Ms Gayens. I apologise.'

'No need to apologise.' Pravi shut the door, leaving Opeia to deal with a number of pressing matters. A number of documents had to be sent through to Rani, who was in the next cabin, trying to get up to date with the business end of things. Promotions to be approved; salary increases to be signed off; new business opportunities to be considered; obsolescent business enterprises to be closed down and information to be sorted and acted upon. It seemed so much. While in transit and away from Earth, comms were difficult or delayed so it paid to get as much in order as possible with regards to the Earth-based operations.

'That's the last of it Rani,' she said into her comms unit just over an hour later. Opeia floated out of her chair and tried to stretch her back. Her gaze slid over the bulkhead. A shower would be nice. Was there a massage bot in her cabin? She thought she'd requested one. There it was.

The door chimed. 'Yes?'

Polly hovered there, dressed in a slim-fitting hot pink ship suit, her short cropped hair dyed bright red. The combination of hair and suit hurt the eyes. It was hard to believe that she was only five years younger than

Opeia. She looked so trendy and sleek, whereas…Opeia looked down at her grey-coloured coverall, she was drab. 'I sent the last lot of correspondence through to you. Also, the list of charity donations for you to approve.'

Opeia groaned. 'I thought it was all done.'

'Sorry. That was Rani's stuff.'

'Will none of it keep?'

'I only dealt with the pressing stuff. There will be stacks when we make the space station and even more when we come back.'

'All right.' Opeia went back to her workstation. Polly hovered close by in case there were any clarifications required.

'Did you see your new bodyguard?' Polly asked with a mischievous gleam in her eye.

'I could not fail to. Why?'

Polly shook her head. 'Nothing. But Rani is being very chatty with him.'

'Her work is done. She has time to fraternise.'

Polly laughed. 'As if you ever cared for that yourself.'

Opeia's head jerked up and she narrowed her gaze. 'What are you saying? That I didn't notice? That I have no…' She shook her head, a smile forming. *Don't go there.*

'Obviously you notice, but were you actually interested?'

'A young thing like that? At my age? Don't be silly.'

Polly gaped at her. 'Ms Gayens. Not only are you a very rich woman, which is alluring on its own to some people, but you are attractive too. If only you'd work at it a bit more.'

'Polly will you get out of here. You're teasing me. It's because I said yes to dinner with McDevitt isn't it?'

Polly grinned at her as she backed away. 'Well, maybe. I will think on something special for you to wear. No daggy shipsuits or pastel-coloured pantsuits which make you look like a grandma or a politician and we have to do something with your hair.'

Opeia patted her hair. 'What's wrong with it?'

'Nothing, you have plenty. It just needs jazzing up a bit.'

'Right. Go get yourself buckled in. We are leaving in less than half an hour.'

Later, showered, massaged to within an inch of her life and strapped in her seat on the main deck, Opeia closed her eyes waiting for the launch. Rani chatted to Pravi, who was strapped in behind Opeia. Riley was on the second deck, with three of his men. Mueller was dictating into his handheld as the Captain counted down. The navigator, Emilie Randall, called back responses on system checks. Although Opeia could run this ship herself on automatic, she had hired a crew. Last time she'd gone solo, she had left herself open to attack. This time she listened to her security team. She just prayed that they would be safe. She would hate to have these lives on her hands. But she couldn't do it herself. She learned that lesson the hard way.

Chapter Four

Disaster Date

The docking procedure at Space Station Beta C went off smoothly. A packet of correspondence came through once they had successfully connected up to space station facilities. Her first appointment was already at the airlock. Opeia rubbed her forehead trying to erase the fatigue. After the jumpgates, she was usually worse for wear. This time someone had used her stomach as a basketball and won the game.

Polly came in and surveyed her. 'You look like crap.'

'Thanks. What's next?' Opeia signed off another contract.

'Another meeting. This one's a politician. McDevitt is up for tonight for dinner.'

'McDevitt?' Opeia puzzled over the name. It rang big bells. 'Oh?'

'Looks to me with your schedule you won't have time to shop.'

'Shop?' Frowning, Opeia glanced up. 'I have everything I need.'

Polly rolled her eyes. 'No, you don't. You don't have an outfit for dinner.'

Opeia leant back and studied her assistant. 'I have plenty of clothes. I'll just wear a ship...no a pantsuit. Perfectly acceptable. It's not like it's a real date.'

Polly grinned evilly. 'I think it is a 'real' date.' She did the finger parentheses. 'Let me do the hard yards. Space City is a fabulous mall. I'll organise a body enhancement too, hair, nail and skin scrub.'

Opeia sunk down in her chair. 'You go too far. Besides I feel comfortable in a pantsuit. The tunic top covers things.'

'Sure you do, but the pantsuits are blah! You need something that will send McDevitt's eyes rolling back in his head. An image he'll never forget.'

Appalled, Opeia laid down the law. 'I'm the boss here.'

'Sure you are.' The door cut off Polly's laugh.

Rani buzzed her. 'The Right Honourable Cora Von Krisp is here for her appointment.'

'Sure, let her through. And bring your handheld I want you in on this one.'

***

The image in the mirror scared Opeia. 'I don't see what's wrong with my hair as it normally is. It's perfectly functional.' She usually wore it cut straight in a bob that curled below her ears. Admittedly it had grown out since her last cut.

The hired hairdresser with hair teased into a big, blue ball, loomed in the mirror, brandishing a long comb. 'You have great colour, Madame, but this rinse will bring out the highlights.'

Buried under a pile of mud on her face, Opeia did her best not to suffocate. 'Polly? Help me, please?'

Polly leant over her shoulder and grinned at her reflection in the mirror. 'The dress I bought for you is great. So fab!' Polly tapped on the hardening mask. 'I think you're almost done.' She drew away and added. 'Perri here is going to do your nails and your makeup too.'

'Please, Polly. I'll give you a raise. Anything. Just let me out of here in one piece.'

'You already gave me a pay rise. Who would have thought that the top exec of AllEarth Corp had no pluck?'

Annoyed, Opeia squeezed the arms of her chair and growled.

'New Earth Woman magazine has been after me for an interview. I could tell them all about your fear of being prettied up.'

'You dare!' Her outrage came out muffled due to the hardened, clay mask.

Polly laughed. Opeia's quarters on the ship were in chaos, with beauty paraphernalia all over the place, shoe boxes, dresses, makeup kits, mirrors. 'I hope McDevitt is worth all this.'

'I'm sure he will be.'

'I can pretty much guarantee that no man is worth this. Why am I doing it?'

As her voice had an authentic sound of desperation in it, Polly patted the top of her hand. 'There, there. How about some coffee?' Polly quipped.

Opeia just groaned as the beautician had started to break apart the mud mask on her face with something that resembled a chisel.

***

Later as she stood by the mirror, Opeia wanted to run.

'Now, because you are on free time, you're Opi now. Get it?' Polly said as she smoothed the dress and surveyed Opeia in the mirror.

'Yeah, right. More like Dopey. I can't do this.' She turned to her aide. 'Let me wear a pantsuit. They are so me.'

'They are so Ms Opeia Gayens, boring business woman. This is Opi.' Polly gestured at the reflection, like she was a rabbit jumping out of a top hat. 'Hot woman looking for love.'

'No! Be serious. I'm not!'

'Just Opi then?' Polly's sleek eyebrows arched.

Opeia capitulated. 'Yes, Opi it is. But,' Opi lifted a lecturing finger. 'I'm docking the expenses for the therapy sessions I'm going to need after tonight from your end of year bonus.' Opi relaxed back into her chair, resigned to her fate. 'By the way, you and the team take the night off, paint the space station red or whatever that expression is.'

Polly grinned. 'All sorted. I am your social secretary after all. I snagged Pravi for a night at the New Ritzo.'

'He's my bodyguard.'

Polly frowned. 'But you don't want him. I thought you and Mueller fought it out and you won.'

Opi grinned. 'I did win. Don't exhaust him. I may need him tomorrow.'

Polly had the beauty technician, Perri, doing her makeup for ages. She felt ridiculous. Her eyelids were smudged with dark brown, her lips a vibrant red. 'I can't do this.' Her litany was even sounding boring to her own ears.

Polly stood back and surveyed Opi's reflection in the mirror, reaching out to adjust the little hat she'd purchased to go with the dress. 'You look great. I haven't seen you in anything but pantsuits and coveralls for years. I can't believe it's you. You're going to knock him dead.'

A smile escaped Opi as she critically surveyed herself in the mirror. 'Do you think the petticoat is too much? The *frou frou* is so 'look at me'.'

Polly motioned for Opi to turn around. Opi did so and the skirt did an amazing twirl. The space station's light gravity made the skirt flutter to her knees in slow motion. 'That style is perfect for you. It nips you in at the waist, hides your butt in the skirt and gracefully draws the eye to your breasts. Perfect.'

'I'm having second thoughts.'

'Too late. Think of it is as a hostile takeover. Go in there, grab all you can take and run.

Opi huffed out a laugh. 'Shoes?'

Polly pulled out red, high-heeled pumps. 'Now these are the best that money can buy and designed for low gravity.' The heels were shiny, metal spikes and Opi could see there was tech in them.

'Are they shoes or weapons?' Opi shook her head. 'I can't possibly walk in them. I'll be crippled before I reach the table.'

Polly laughed as she put them on the ground. 'No, you won't. They are designed for low gravity. If you have problems with traction, you just have to engage this button on the top of the heel and an attraction field will engage.'

'What good is that?'

Polly studied her face. 'I don't know. It seemed like a good idea at the time. They look great don't they?' She grimaced. 'Well, they work in microgravity but I guess you'd hardly be wearing high heels at a time like that.' She picked one up and pretended to throw it. 'A weapon perhaps. In case your date gets frisky.'

'It's not a really a date. It's business related.' Opi squeezed her foot into the shoes, then looked up to see Polly's cocked disbelieving eyebrow. 'Okay it's sort of a date. The butterflies in my stomach tell me it's a date.'

'Been a long time?'

'Oh yes.'

'Knock him dead.'

The trip to the hotel where she was meeting McDevitt was long. Not in time, but in degrees of embarrassment and sometimes moments of sheer terror. People looked at her. Some openly stared. If she had time, she would have reversed tracks and gone back to her ship to change into something more conservative—a nice comfortable cream-coloured pantsuit, flat-heeled shoes. Totally unobjectionable clothing.

As it was she stood in the foyer of the hotel, with the restaurant through the large opening to her right, contemplating a retreat. Subdued lighting, white table cloths on tables set a good distance apart proved that the eating establishment was high end as space was expensive on a space station like this.

Opi ran a nervous hand down her retro dress, with its tight waist and flared skirt in flamboyant red. She looked like she'd stepped out of a 1950s' movie. Her handheld was sitting in its pouch on the side of her bra. A little pill box hat sat on the side of her head and her hair was twirled up into a chignon and decorated with little porcelain roses. The hairdo was much more elaborate than she was used to. It called attention to itself, something she'd never needed to do. She was usually trying to be inconspicuous and that never worked either. People could smell money.

The restaurant in the *Hotel Magnifique* spanned the lower side of Space Station Beta C just below the centre line and provided a full view of the jumpgates beyond. The star field was muted by the large floor to ceiling windows a good two floors high. Industrial-sized viewscreens if Opi knew her interstellar construction standards. Arranged along the windows were smooth, metal pylons appearing decorative but were actually part of the support structure.

The maitre'd bowed to her. He was dressed in immaculate black tie. 'Monsieur McDevitt is already here. If you will follow me.' He spoke with what Opi decided was a genuine French accent. Impressed, she followed along, paying as much attention to her shoes and how she walked as she could without staring at her feet. They were not as painful as she thought they would be, but they were different to her usual sensible flats. Her weight being augmented by the low gravity, she did not twist an ankle. That did not, however, make them any easier to walk in.

On nearing the table, Opi had the impulse to turn and run. What did she think she was doing, dressed up like some...some woman who wanted a man? Had she taken leave of her senses? Too late, the *maitre'd* stepped aside. McDevitt rose to his feet. He was taller than her even in the heels. The suit of grey fitted him like a glove as his well-muscled torso filled it creditably. She wanted to squeeze his biceps to see if they were real. The black shirt he wore beneath it was opened at his tanned throat. He opened his mouth to speak, but paused. His gaze flitted over her outfit and then centred on her face. 'You're Opeia Gayens?' he sounded doubtful, like the waiter had presented a pleasure bot or something and not Opeia Gayens.

Trying to hide the fact that she was disconcerted by his reaction and that she was likely to fall out of her shoes at any moment, she plonked herself on the chair held out for her. 'Yes. That's me. How do you do?'

She checked the position of the pill box hat on her head and smiled.

He still stood there transfixed, his blue eyes locked onto her face. His tan complexion paled. 'The Opeia Gayens?'

Gazing up at him from her seat. 'You were expecting me?'

'Yes...but...' Then recollecting himself, he thanked the *maitre'd* and asked for the *Bollinger* to be served before taking his seat.

There was this awkward moment when neither of them spoke. Opi figured she had failed the date before she began. He was obviously repulsed by her. Disappointed, maybe.

He sat down. 'Forgive me,' he said. 'You aren't what I expected.'

'I'm not sure how to take that. Should I just go now?' She made to move out of the chair.

He put out a hand. 'No. Don't go. I'm sorry.' He studied her face. 'It's just that you remind me of someone I once knew. The resemblance is so uncanny. Well...it is a bit of a shock.'

'I do keep my personal image out of the media as much as I can but it's impossible to keep it out completely. Do you mean you don't recognise me at all? I had thought...'

His gaze drifted down. 'Yes, in general I do recognise you. But in person I see...' His brows furrowed. 'Perhaps the dress... You look younger than I expected.' His cheeks turned red.

Opi looked down at her clothing. 'You don't like it?' Maybe she should leave. This was a big mistake. Her cheeks burned. Now they both were suffering from acute embarrassment. Why didn't life have replay buttons like the vids? She'd really like to redo her entrance, her clothing choices and damn...maybe even saying yes to dinner.

McDevitt sat back, his eyebrows flying high. 'Oh no. I mean I love the dress. You look amazing...Have you had your body and face altered recently?'

'What? No! You've got a nerve. Are you trying to be insulting?'

'No! No,' he replied in a less panicked voice, raising his hands to ward of her ire. A waiter appeared with the *Bollinger* and filled their flute tubes. She took a sip, thinking it was time to leave, perhaps after the champagne. *Of all the nerve.* She should have guessed McDevitt was out to insult her. So much for being grateful she left him a planet in her takeover. Too soft by half.

He glanced up at her warily after placing his champagne tube back in its holder. 'I meant no insult. Really I didn't. People get body enhancements all the time. I thought perhaps that your resemblance was accidental.' He shrugged. 'I'm thrown that's all.'

Opi blinked and had a growing sense of disquiet. 'Someone living?'

McDevitt's blue eyes lowered to the table top. He played with the stem of his champagne flute tube. 'No, she's gone.'

'I'm sorry.' Opeia looked around the room avoiding his gaze. Talk about awkward. *Great!* She reminded him of a dead person. She wanted to go back to her quarters on her ship and eat a double size sundae with chocolate and caramel topping and a whole pint of whipped cream.

'Look. I'm sorry for my reaction. Truly. Can we start again? I realise I made you feel uncomfortable and that was never my intention.'

Her gaze centred on him. He lifted his lips in a smile and his eyes danced as they met hers. 'What do you say? Start again?'

'Sure. Okay.' She put out her hand. 'Please to meet you Mr McDevitt. Please call me Opeia.'

He inclined his head. 'Thank you. Please call me Owain.'

She repeated his name to test out the pronunciation.

With a grin, he signalled the waiter. 'I hope you don't mind but I've ordered the degustation menu. This restaurant is famous for it. I've not been here before. It was on my must do list. Besides meeting you that is.'

'That is...perfectly fine, Mr McDevitt.'

'Owain.'

Her cheeks flushed. 'Oh...yes...sorry...I'm...I'm...' Could she do it? Be Opi? Not Opeia? He gazed at her, his lips parted, left eyebrow slightly raised. He thought her daft.

'Call me Opi. Do you mind?' She let out a big breath. 'I mean my friends call me Opi.' Actually it was only her daughter Rae, and now Polly, that cheeky little assistant of hers.

'Opi? That sounds lovely.' He bowed his head and then smiled. 'I'm honoured.'

She returned his smile. He was attractive, in a rugged sort of way she supposed. But it was ridiculous. She had no idea why she was there. Curiosity? Boredom? Looking for something different in her life?

'The food will be here soon. I want to thank you again for letting me repay, in some small way, your great kindness to me.'

His blue eyes fixed on her and she returned his gaze and then dropped it to the plate and said to herself. 'Mmm.' He was charming, that's for sure. Sort of took her breath away. And his attention made her squirm. She was tempted to pull out her handheld and start doing some business, just to avoid being so exposed. No props. Just her and him. *Weird.*

Perhaps the food would be a distraction. Opi relaxed as the first course was served and eyed it with anticipation. On the small plate set before her was some kind of slug in an aromatic garlic sauce. Fighting hard to keep the disappointment showing on her face, she broke off some bread and dipped it into the sauce. No way was she actually going to eat the slimy things but she could be adventurous and taste the edges of the dish. Cautiously, she bit into the bread and the flavours of butter and garlic filled her mouth. With a smile of relief, she swallowed. That was about all she could manage in the eating stakes.

While McDevitt ate his space slugs, Opi studied him. There was no sign of hesitation in eating the food. Strong stomach or used to eating slugs? Or was he putting on a brave front? If that was the case he was doing a good job of hiding any distaste.

He started talking about his journey from Islay 2. McDevitt used his utensils efficiently. No waving them about as he talked, just rested them on the edge of his plate. His tanned hands were square and strong, the nails neatly trimmed. His jaw also was squarish and his complexion smooth. He had a top grade depilatory device she guessed or he had his beard permanently removed. His eyes were wide and startling blue under strong dark eyebrows. There was a smattering of grey in his hair, just above the ears. Natural, she thought, not an affectation.

The waiter interrupted McDevitt talking about his agricultural activities when he placed two tubes of wine before them. Opi couldn't help thinking that potatoes and dirt were dull and owned herself a snob. She had dedicated her life to eating potatoes not growing them.

McDevitt chatted to the waiter about the wine selection. His eyelids lowered as he studied her plate as it was taken away. He'd seen she didn't eat her slugs. Well, if that offended him there was nothing she could do about it. She smiled vacantly and cast her gaze about the room, thinking this whole deal had been a mistake. She tried to keep that knowledge out of her expression. It took a great deal of her business skills to do that. If this had been a business meeting going this badly she would have called it quits. But this was a date and she didn't want to offend McDevitt. After all she had been nice to him once apparently. Why spoil that?

With a great deal of pageantry and napkin waving, the next course was delivered. Her interest was aroused. Her stomach rumbled and she hoped he didn't hear it. The plate was placed in front of her. On it was a small tart with something she couldn't identify in it. 'What is it?' she asked, forgetting to be non-judgmental.

McDevitt picked up the small menu that had been propped in the middle of the table. 'Torte d'intestins a la mode.''

Opi glared at her plate. 'Is that what I think it is?'

'Guts?' He nodded. 'Well-seasoned though.' He inhaled theatrically. 'Delicious.'

Opi decided that business skills weren't going to work. How soon could she get out of this fiasco and order up a pizza in her suite on her ship?

She picked up her fork, studied her plate and her plan of attack and sighed.

'Is there something wrong with your food?' He asked, a faint smile around his eyes.

She put the fork down carefully and rested her chin in her folded hands. 'Do you want an honest answer? Or the company line?'

'The honest answer, of course. Always.'

'Be careful what you wish for. I can't eat this tripe.'

He inclined his head, snorted out a laugh and then composed himself. 'This restaurant has a great rep.'

'I don't care what reputation it has. They probably paid for it.'

He chuckled and looked out the viewport, his face suddenly thoughtful. He was probably looking for a way to get out of the dinner too. What a disaster.

However, Opi was here and she was hungry. 'Do you mind if I order something else?'

McDevitt turned back to her, slight surprise on his face. His intestine pie untouched. He dropped his fork onto his plate with a clang. He studied her, blue eyes glittering, then barked out a laugh. 'I can't believe you read my mind.' He lifted a hand. 'Waiter!'

The waiter came over. 'Cancel the degustation menu, will you?' He lifted an eyebrow at Opi. 'Steak?'

'Yes!' To the waiter she said. 'New York cut, medium rare. Salad and garlic fries.'

'The same.'

The waiter looked down his nose, then picked up the small plates and walked away.

McDevitt looked at her, lifted an eyebrow and Opi burst out laughing. She pulled off her hat and tossed it on the floor at her feet. 'What a mistake that was.'

'But it looks so good on you.' McDevitt reached under the table to collect it, dusted it off and then placed it gently on the edge of the table. 'I'm sorry about the food. I thought you'd be impressed with my taste.'

Opi couldn't keep the smile off her face. 'That's funny.' She gestured at the dress. 'This wasn't my idea, but I suppose I was hoping to do some impressing too.'

He nodded, as if understanding and then sighed, his eyes on the star field on the other side of the viewport.

No point in trying to impress anyone anymore. The cat was definitely out of the bag. She plonked an elbow on the table and rested her chin on it. 'Do you mind awfully if I slipped off these abominable shoes?'

He turned back to her, laugh lines crinkling around his eyes. 'Of course not. I want you to be comfortable, easy around me. Shall I take them off for you?' He lifted the table cloth, head dipping sideways as if he intended on doing the deed.

'No! No, I can manage. I think my assistant thought I could use them to protect myself.' She lifted one, made a pretend throw so he could see. 'Full of tech and all that jazz.'

His right eyebrow rose, followed by the left. 'You could certainly harm someone with those if you tried.'

Her stomach rumbled again and she spotted his untouched bread roll. 'Do you mind if I eat that? I think the steaks may take a while.'

He passed the bread roll to her and she ripped it apart and demolished it and took a sip of the wine from the glass tube. 'Not bad,' she commented lifting her drink in salute.

He let out a sigh and collapsed against his seat. 'I got one thing right. Although, it was the restaurant that chose the wine. I drink single malt whisky mostly. Don't know much about wine at all.'

She giggled and sipped the wine again. 'Tell me, do you often proposition female industrialists or is this your first time?'

He shook his head, eyes wide and mouth aghast. 'I didn't realise I had 'propositioned' you. I asked you to dine with me. I've met my share of powerful women of industry. Not that any were as surprising as you. Anyway I was happily married for fifteen years so my invitation technique is a little rusty.'

Opi blinked and grinned, pleased that he was being candid with her. Then she sobered, remembering that he was a widower. 'What happened?'

'She died. Organ failure after an accident.'

'That's unusual.' With even basic medical facilities she should have been revivable. There was more to it, she supposed.

'It was.'

'Children?' She asked, but she remembered reading in his profile that he had.

'A daughter, Lucinda. She's at home, on Islay 2. She's fourteen. You?'

'Ah...you probably read the headlines. I can't imagine you haven't done at least a basic netsearch and I know what comes up when you do.'

'I have. I'm sorry you had such a bad time of it. Two daughters, now. Independent?'

'Yes. They aren't interested in the company or the money. I don't know where I went wrong. I lucked out on instilling in them the need for money, for greed, for world domination...'

He chuckled, getting in tune with her humour. 'Maybe you didn't go wrong.'

She sighed. 'Yes, maybe I wish I was more like them. I envy them their freedom, freedom to choose. It makes me wonder about myself and the decisions I did and did not make.'

The smell of fries reached her and she sat up, eyes wide. A huge plate was placed in front of her. A sizzling New York cut steak, a mountain of fries and a small bowl of salad greens. Just what she'd ordered. *Perfect.*

It was real cow, not the fake stuff. As she cut into it and shoved a slice into her mouth, her stomach fluttered and her plate rose above the table slightly before settling again. She gulped down her mouthful, eyes narrowing. 'That's a glitch in the gravity.'

McDevitt surveyed the room. 'Other diners have noticed it. No panic though. Maybe it's normal for this space station.'

Opi shook her head. Gravity generation was a big deal. That felt like the spin generator had gone onto back up power. 'Damn it! I'm eating this steak whether there is a malfunction or not.'

The chairs and the tables were secured to the floor. She put a hand on her plate to steady it in case of further fluctuations. She was not losing one of her fries to the atmosphere.

Opi swallowed another slice of steak and jammed in some fries. Too late for dainty eating. A steak was involved now. This 'date' was already a disaster so some straight talking, no nonsense bad table manners weren't going to change anything. Although, McDevitt seemed to be taking the whole date debacle well, given the way he too was tucking into the food.

After making very short work of the bulk of her meal, she eased back in her chair and belched. Her hand covered her mouth and her eyes rounded. She hadn't meant for that to slip out. 'Oops, sorry.'

McDevitt gaped at her. 'Did you?...was that?' He burst out laughing. 'Famous.'

He leant forward and squeezed her hand. 'You, Ms Gayens are not what I expected. I mean Opi. I thought you would be an uptight, upper class...ultra rich...uber...'

Opi covered her mouth to hide a champagne burp chasing the steak one. It could not be repressed. 'Well, I am uptight usually...Not really upper class whatever that is, but I can be classified as ultra rich. I'm not normally noted for being a 'bitch'. Well, not to my face.' She did the air parenthesis then narrowed her eyes, noting his surprise. 'That's what you were going to say wasn't it?'

'Yes.' He leant forward. 'But I didn't think you were, because you didn't take Islay 2 when I know you could have. That's why I wanted to meet you. I was intrigued. And I wanted to thank you personally.'

'And now you've met me? In all my glory.' She sat back and threw out her hands, indicating her hot red dress and the *frou frou* skirt and petticoat. Maybe the champagne and wine had gone to her head. She wasn't normally so daring, so free.

He opened his mouth and then looked about him. He was floating off his chair. Opi was too.

'The gravity?' she said, waving her arms about trying to get a grip on something. She snatched at the edge of the table and missed. Stupid to take off her shoes, they had tech in them for situations like these.

Yells and screams and crashes echoed around them as the other patrons and staff experienced the effects of microgravity. No hazard alarm blared. That was odd. There should have been a warning.

Opi floated higher. Not good. Not if the gravity came back. McDevitt had snagged a nearby pylon with his foot and climbed up so he could grab hold of her. He groped for her a few times and missed. Her dress was not microgravity friendly. The skirt and petticoat fluffed up around her upper body and she had to push it away to see where she was and try to push it down to cover her panties.

A hand on her foot and she squeaked. 'It's me,' McDevitt said. His other hand grabbed her calves.

'Ooh!'

Thankfully, she had very nice stockings on. He drew her closer to the pylon as he reeled her in.

'Don't worry I've got you.' Another hand came up to draw her down. He spat out a mouthful of skirt. 'We've got to get closer to the floor or we could get hurt if they restart the spin.'

'The gravity generator is out? How?' The space station had internal spin, plus a network of attraction fields to simulate gravity. Not Earth full gravity but about sixty per cent.

'I don't know but it's not good.'

His hands were on her upper thighs just below the curve of her buttocks. 'Eep! What are you doing?' It was disturbing having his strong hands just there.

'Trying to bring you in. This dress of yours is…difficult.' His voice was muffled with tulle.

Opi was near suffocating in the wide skirt that covered her lower face. She was trying to decide whether to push it down for modesty's sake or make a grab for the pylon. Warm breath brushed against the sensitive area of her crotch. A spike of something she didn't recognise lanced up through to her heart. A jolt of electricity? He breathed again and his chin or nose pressed into her sex with the same titillating sensation. 'Jesus, what are you doing?' Opi was so embarrassed she wanted to die. She tried to get away. McDevitt had a hold of her. 'Don't kick me, damn it. I'm trying to help here.'

He put his arm over her leg and now his face was firmly planted in her panties. 'Oh god!' Opi wasn't sure if she was more excited or more embarrassed by her current predicament. Yet, falling suddenly to the floor had more serious consequences.

'Grab hold of me with your other leg. Can you find my shoulder?'

'What?' Consigning herself to the gods, she looped her leg around his shoulder. 'Is that it?'

'Yes.' He eased her leg down and guided it around his waist. They were almost face to face, except for the *frou frou* of her dress.

He slid down the pylon bringing them to the ground. Pushing the petticoat out of her face, she rasped. 'Can you help me with this damn nuisance dress?'

'Sure.' He grabbed hold of some fabric in one hand. 'This has to go.' There was a tug and then a tear. Her petticoat floated away.

'Oh there you are.' She could see his face.

'Give me your hand.' She put her hand in his, frowning in consternation.

'If I can get to my shoes they have an attraction field. I could walk on my own then.'

'Right.' Their table was close. She stretched out to try to reach them while still being held by McDevitt.

Overhead warning lights flashed ominously. The intercom blared. 'Warning, warning. Gravity resumes in five, four, three, two, one...'

Opi's weight grew on her too suddenly. She was slapped against the floor. McDevitt landed on her. She half turned to see his nose pressed into her butt. 'Great.' Glad she'd taken some 'No Gas' before the meal, otherwise more than her dress would be red.

She lifted up trying to dislodge him. He supported himself on two hands and shook his head.

He slapped her butt and it wobbled. 'Thanks for the soft-landing.' Then he pulled out his comms unit and started muttering urgently into it.

Opi decided she never wanted to see McDevitt again. How could she? After the disasters of the evening? What man in his right mind wanted to date someone like her, clueless and clumsy and with a wobbly butt. Not to mention digestion issues. Although she was not normally this way, in business, surrounded by her team, she was able to pull it off. She obviously needed some social training before embarking on the dating game.

The warning lights stopped flashing. Sitting on the ground, she slid her feet into her shoes. Then using the pylon for support she climbed to her feet and peered out the viewport.

Catching her eye were faint flashes around the docking ports on this side of the space station. McDevitt's voice was low as he spoke into his comms unit. A grunt signalled the end of the conversation. She swung around. Her comms unit was in her clutch purse. She had to remember to get it when she left. McDevitt swung her back around to face him. 'What?'

His eyes glittered as he held her by the shoulders, then ran his hands down her body. 'What are you doing?' His mouth twisted and he ripped the skirt from the waist of her dress. She thumped him on the shoulder. 'Are you crazy? What did you do that for?'

He put his face close to hers. 'We are under attack. We need to leave now.' He spoke each word slowly and clearly as if she was an idiot. But as the words sunk in, her stomach tightened.

'Attack?' The flashes outside the viewport were growing brighter and closer. 'But this is Space Station Beta C. Who would attack it? It's too well protected and armoured. I saw the specs myself. I nearly hit my security chief over the head with them just so he wouldn't do cavity searches on you and have my bodyguard share our dinner.'

He blinked at her, taking that rapid flow of information in. 'Space pirates...'

'No, way. It's too big, too well guarded.'

He turned her around and faced her to the viewport. An explosive burst of flame arced out of the docking port. Then the trembling vibration reached the steel under their feet.

'But...it's too soon.'

His brows furrowed. 'What's too soon? Look, I'm in contact with my ship. It's in the docking bay on the far side. It's not under attack, yet.'

'Then the docking port where my ship is under attack?'

He grimaced. Opi dived for her clutch purse and dug out her comms and shoved it in her ear. 'Polly? Polly do you read?'

Nothing but static. 'Mueller? Give me status? Hello?'

She tried the ship direct. 'Captain Graves? Do you read me? What is your status?' Not even static. 'Bugger and blast.'

'Come on. We best get moving. I'm keyed into the station security system. There are armed intruders heading in this direction.'

A wave of dizziness hit her. 'Intruders?' This should not be happening.

'Yes.' He took her elbow to lead her away. 'Right. Okay. Let's go.'

Chapter Five

Into the Access Chute

'How come you are linked into security? My research said you were retired.' She followed along with him, his hand warm against her bare forearm.

'I'm retired.' He drew out a small tool kit, took out a screw driver and undid the wall panel. She stepped back to give him some room and watched as he stuck his head in the space behind. Another grunt as he withdrew from his inspection of the chute. Then McDevitt grabbed her by the elbow and pulled her toward the opening. 'You first.'

'Stop manhandling me.' She pushed at his hands that seemed to be everywhere.

'Hurry, damn it! We don't want them to know how we escaped.'

'Why would they care?' She grumbled as she got in. Her shoes were no help so she slipped them off and carried them as she crawled. They *thunked, thunked* on the metal base of the access crawl way. Not having the skirt made it easier to crawl. But she didn't like the idea of McDevitt peering at her butt, now nicely framed in her pale pink panties and the ragged strips that were the remains of her the skirt of her dress. He'd already been overly familiar with her nether regions as it was. Her dignity had gone out the bloody air lock. She half turned in the small space and watched him reattach the panel after he'd climbed in behind her.

He looked over his shoulder. 'What are you waiting for? Move!' his voice was not over loud but it held a tone of command.

'Where am I going?'

He crawled after her. 'I studied the schematics before I came. Turn left.'

She blinked as she crawled as fast as she could 'That's a bit paranoid isn't it? You studied the whole space station's specs?'

'No. Not paranoid when you are taking one of the richest women in our part of space out to dinner.'

'Don't be ridiculous. It has to be paranoid.'

He scowled at her, barring his teeth. 'It's not ridiculous.'

'But nobody but my team knows—'

'Keep moving.' He prodded her on the behind.

'Hey!' she protested. 'Keep your hands off my ass.'

'You have a leak.'

She paused, concern making her face flush, then she realised not that kind of leak. 'Blast you. I do not.' Only her inner circle knew about the dinner. Surely, it hadn't been one of them. It must be a leak somewhere else. Her system could be compromised, but it wasn't likely. She could afford the best in system security. A nervous twinge clenched her gut. If it had been betrayal, she was seriously stuffed. She didn't think she had it in her to face the space pirates again. Not dressed like this.

'How do I know whoever they are aren't after you?'

She heard him sigh. 'Because I haven't declared war on the space pirates. You have. I have more subtlety.'

'So you really think it's space pirates attacking this station?'

'No one has the man power, the guts and the sheer desperation.'

The grey metal corridor split in three directions. 'Which way?'

The gravity died again and this time the change made her feel sick. She rolled her eyes. This date could not get any worse. If she ralphed she was going to give up men forever. They weren't worth the embarrassment. Traction under her hands and knees was difficult without the bonus of gravity. She had to pull and push herself off the walls. Glancing back or down, she was confused now. She noticed McDevitt seemed in control of himself. He caught her eye. 'You okay?'

She ground her teeth. 'I'm coping.' She put her hand to her belly as it flopped over. She nearly stabbed herself with the heels of her shoes. 'I need to speak to my team.'

'No. Don't try them again. It's dangerous.' He put out his hand. 'Better still, give me your link.'

'But...but'

'Give it over.' He had his hand out flat, then lifted his fingers encouragingly. 'Come on.'

She clutched her link protectively. 'No. Why would I do that?' Her handheld was in her body purse. Not easy to get to while fully clothed in company.

'So you don't get tempted. They could be tracking it. Watch out!'

The ground opened up under her. Lucky the gravity was off, but it was enough to send her bouncing off one wall and into another. She had to duck to miss hitting herself in the head with her shoes. McDevitt grabbed her and held her still. 'We go down.' He held out his other hand. 'Carefully. Use the hand grips. Link.'

Looking up into his face, she had the oddest sensation and smiled at him. 'How do I know I can trust you? I don't even know you. If I was paranoid I would think this is a set up.'

He rolled his eyes. 'It is rather an elaborate plot, where my communications are on record inviting you here.'

'Records can be erased.' He shook his head and plucked her comms unit out of her hand. He switched it off and said, 'Down.'

'Well?' She held the shoes in one hand and had her other hand free for hand grips. She thought of putting them back on but not in these access tubes.

'I have records at my end, as well as the comms station relay buffers in a direct path to Earth. A good cop would know where to look.'

She looked down. 'Do I go slowly or push off? If I push off and the gravity comes back on I'm toast. Squashed toast.'

'Push off, but be ready to brace. It's narrow enough that you could put out both hands and feet and lock onto the wall if gravity comes back up. We need the third access port on the right. Got it?'

She waved the shoes at him and he rolled his eyes again.

'Go.'

'Yes. Okay.' Opi pushed off and down, using occasional hand grips to correct her path and push off. The distance between the access ports was quite long.

Just past the second one the walls trembled and she hit her head a glancing blow and bounced back. Shaking herself, she put her free arm to the wall, seeking a hand hold in case the gravity came back on. McDevitt ploughed into her and they tangled, arms and legs, until he found a hand hold and stopped them.

He grabbed the heel of one of her shoes. 'Why don't you ditch these stupid things?'

'Because I can use them in the corridors. They have an attraction field built in.'

He shook his head. 'Keep them under control before they take someone's eye out.'

She gave him a withering look and pushed downwards.

The third access port was just below their feet.

He looked her over and he frowned. 'You're bleeding,' he said reaching out to touch her head. Drawing closer, he inspected the wound. 'It's not too deep. Must have hurt when you did that. You feel okay?'

'You keep asking if I'm okay.' She pushed away his hands. 'I'm not okay. All right?' Her emotions and fear had joined together. 'I'm pissed... and now I'm bleeding and the bloody damn dress that Polly bought me from Star City Mall is totally ruined...' She waved a shoe at him.

McDevitt pushed off, snagging her arm and swung her into the access port. 'No time for tantrums just now.'

With the momentum she had, Opi couldn't get a hold of anything and she kept going through the port.

McDevitt caught her by the foot. 'Not so fast. This is where we exit.'

She looked along her body at him. 'You know what. I feel like kicking you in the face right now.'

He laughed. 'I know just how you feel. This was not the way I expected the evening to go either.'

'Really. What did you expect?'

He opened the port door and shrugged. 'I don't know. I thought you must be a nice person and that it would be good to find out how nice. You aren't what I expected.'

Opi hadn't known what to expect either. 'Did you just want to meet me or was it more like a date?'

He glanced over his shoulder. 'What do you think?' and he pushed the door open and shoved her through.

Chapter Six

Crawling with Space Pirates

Opi landed, bounced and gaped at her surroundings. It looked like a huge machine room. Atmospheric control perhaps. She shoved her feet into her shoes, engaged the attraction field and climbed erect, grateful to be able to walk again.

McDevitt slid out more gracefully than she had, and paused to check out the room too. He oriented himself and then gradually lowered to the ground. 'There's gravity here. Not normal, but some.'

'The internal spin is slowed.'

'Yeah, the attraction fields are bouncing about. We'd best take it carefully.'

McDevitt walked toward her and snagged her by the elbow. 'We need to keep moving. They are in the restaurant and it's not pretty.'

'How do you know?' she asked, trying to dislodge his arm, then realised he was using her as an anchor.

'I left a micro vid camera on the pylon. The feed is coming through now.' A small eye screen hovered over one eye. He must have had a brow insert for she'd not seen it before.

'Shit. They aren't hurting people are they?'

'No. Most of the patrons are gone, but they are destroying the joint looking for you.'

'But how do you know they want me and how did they know I'd be there? I could have changed my mind about meeting you. Gee, I almost did about five times.'

McDevitt lifted a chin. 'I'm that scary. I'm not sure whether to be pleased or not. This way and watch your head.'

The covered passage way was low. Fit only for repair bots, she thought. She had to squat down and waddle along. 'It might be easier to crawl.' McDevitt said from behind her.

She turned to face him. 'Why? So you can ogle my butt some more?'

He pursed his lips and tilted his head. 'That has to be a perk of the job.'

'I'm a job?'

'Turn of phrase. Actually at his moment I am saving your ass so keep moving. Watch out!'

Opi ducked down just in time. 'Goddamit there is moving machinery in here. Are you trying to kill me?' She was gliding sideways so could send him a good glare.

He rolled his eyes. 'Not far now. Then we run for it.'

She looked down at her shoes and thought about the gravity. Maybe he was being metaphorical.

They climbed out onto an access ramp. 'Hit the release on that door.'

Opi smacked it with a growl. 'Which way?'

'Left.'

She faced that direction. A long straight corridor was ahead of her. She tried to orient herself. 'Crew quarters?'

McDevitt placed himself in front of her and checked the corridor behind and cast a glance back the way they had come. 'We have to hurry. Gravity is off again. Disengage your shoes.'

Opi leant down and turned off the attraction field.

McDevitt kicked off the floor, snagged her arm and brought her with him. He bounced and jumped again, like he was used to working in low gravity. Opi concentrated to keeping herself oriented to the vertical and clung to his forearm with both her hands. 'Are they following?'

'I don't know. But if they figure out where my ship is docked then it makes sense they will head there.'

Her stomach dropped. 'That's a big incursion onto a government space station. They must be desperate.'

'They are. But you know that already. Ten to one odds you put some bait out there.'

Opi narrowed her gaze. 'I don't know what you mean. I've been using all available legal channels to get them out of my company.'

He nodded and turned back to concentrate on their route. They rounded a corner. Piles of clothing lay by closed doors. The staff here had obviously been in a hurry when they left their quarters.

He turned her so they were nose to nose. 'You're coming on my ship. If you have any plans that I need to know about you better spill them now.'

Opi lifted her chin. 'I'm not getting on your ship.'

He shook his head. 'Your ship is probably space junk now.'

'No! My crew!'

He groped for her hand and squeezed. 'I'm sure your crew got out okay. Colonel Mueller is a good man.'

'How did you…wait a minute you know him?'

'No, but he called me and read me the lecture on how to treat you and what he'd do to me if anything were to happen. I came prepared.'

'He had no right to do that. I'm sorry.'

McDevitt laughed. 'I'm not. It was better than the cavity search he threatened me with. Now the access to the docking ports is through here. Do you have a weapon?'

'No! They aren't allowed.'

He reached down and pulled out a small pen out of his sock. 'Aren't they?'

'What is that?'

'A laser. Won't last long but enough for a couple of skirmishes.'

The door was locked. The panic was building up again inside. The thought of being captured by the pirates once more started to push into her mind like a wedge. She had to fight to keep the dread out. She didn't want to face that again. This time they'd kill her because she'd changed it all. No codes were going to give them access to anything. They needed living DNA, plus retina scans and voice print.

McDevitt tried a code on the door. It didn't budge. 'They must be in main control. The master code has been overwritten.'

He aimed his laser. 'Bugger this is going to alert them where we are.' He checked up and around. 'Damn, bound to be vid cameras anyway.'

Zapped, the control sizzled and popped. There was a thunk as the door lock released. McDevitt pulled and pushed at the door so it opened enough to let them through. Screaming sounded over loud after the relative quiet of the crews' quarters.

'Mass exodus?' she asked as he tugged her down the docking port corridor.

'I hope so. We can hide in all the confusion.' He checked his bearings. 'This way.' He put the link to his mouth. 'Almost there. Be ready. Go manual on the docking clips. Quiet like.'

'You really can't take me on your ship.'

'No choice, Ms Gayens.'

'It's Opi.'

They turned a corner and bodies were bouncing everywhere. They got separated. Opi didn't know where to go. Then she saw him. Big guy, tattoos and implants all over him. Shaved head. Classic pirate. When he spied her and dove in her direction it confirmed her visual ID.

The gravity was shit. All over the place. It was like trying to run through soup. Opi turned, tried to bounce, but the pirate was there. He had her by the feet. She screamed, a moment of pure terror.

The pirate grinned at her. Then a green-hued, light flashed, momentarily dazzling her. 'I'm here.' McDevitt's arm snaked around her waist. The pirate fell away screaming. His hands still held her ankles, then she kicked her feet in a panic and his severed arms fell away. She screamed again, tears streaking down her face.

'I've got you.' McDevitt kicked off again and then snagged at a door with his free hand. The door slid aside and then he dove through the docking tube into the ship, bringing her with him.

McDevitt shouted once they were on board. 'Now. Now. Now!'

The ship shuddered under her feet. 'I've got to get up on deck. Sorry about the inconvenience.' He shoved her into the emergency netting. 'It's going to be rough. Sorry. Hold on.'

'But!'

He was gone. Entangled in the netting, Opi tried to get free but when the ship began to move, she decided it was best to stay put until the ride smoothed out. Worry over her team loomed large in her mind. Had they all gone on board the station? The loss of the ship didn't concern her. She had her handheld with all her data on it. If only she could get it out now she could contact her ship, check in with Polly, send orders where they needed to go to meet up again.

A sudden jerk of the ship and she was clinging tight to the webbing. Was that a blast? Why would anyone be firing on McDevitt's ship? They knew she was on board? Her heart fluttered uncomfortably.

McDevitt obviously thought the same thing as he appeared in front of her. 'Hand it over!' His face was tight with anger, eyes blazing, lips a straight line.

'What?' Fingers caught in the netting, she leant back, away from his rage.

'Whatever you are using to transmit.' He spoke clearly and slowly.

She answered in kind. 'But I'm not transmitting anything.'

The ship lurched again and McDevitt rode it out, putting his hand on the bulkhead to steady himself.

'You have your handheld?'

'Yes, but it's switched off in my body pack. I haven't touched it.'

He studied her. 'True?'

'Of course it's true.'

'Right then.'

He disentangled her from the webbing and pulled her along further into the ship. 'What are you doing?' She tried to grab something and failed. 'Are you crazy?' Oh please god, don't let him be crazy.

He thumped the wall and a door slid open. He flung her through and her butt hit a medbed. 'Why am I in here?'

'I'm going to scan you for implants.'

'I don't have any implants. That's ridiculous.'

'Humour me. It won't hurt a bit...unless I find one.'

The scanner he held over her beeped. 'Got it in one.'

She covered her arm with a hand. 'Not possible.'

'Entirely possible.' He groped around in a drawer and pulled out something that looked like giant tweezers with entirely too pointy ends. 'Had any shots lately?'

'Just some booster shots for standard diseases last month.'

'Well, Ms Gayens. You got something extra last time.'

He sprayed her upper arm and the skin went dead. 'Don't move.'

A burning pain cut into her skin despite the numbing agent. She held still, even though she wanted to pull away and scream. 'Almost have it.'

There was a tug, a high-level sting which made her cry out and he shouted in triumph. He dropped the little metal device that was the size of a grain of rice into a dish and waved it under her nose. 'Hold that, while I bandage you up.'

Tears rolled down her cheeks and she sniffed. 'It hurts.'

He brushed her hair softly. It had started to come out of the tight bun. 'I know. I'm sorry.'

She glanced up at him, realising he knew what she meant. It wasn't the physical pain as much as the thought of being betrayed. She thought she was over that. But it still happened anyway. People always wanted something from her. Pity that some of them wanted her dead.

Glancing down at McDevitt's handiwork, she saw he was experienced in first aid. He had sealed the wound and covered it in Newskin. 'It's going to hurt for a while. I've got to deal with this.' He took the dish with her tracker in it. 'Why don't you bunk down in my cabin? Come on. You look done in.'

Opi wiped the tip of her nose with the back of her hand. She was feeling very sorry for herself and extremely tired. They had come a long way through the space station. 'All right. Where are we going?' She was feeling woozy.

He put an arm around her waist and supported her out of the tiny sick bay. 'I'll keep that information for myself for now. By the way, I've sedated you. Just in case you had ideas to contact your crew. You'll be asleep for about twelve hours. Don't worry I'll take good care of you.'

'But,' she said as she gazed up at him, shock and dismay in her eyes. 'You too?' She meant had he betrayed her too, but then she was floating on a drug haze.

'I'm sorry, Opi. Trust me.' He caught her, gave her a peck on the lips and carried her into his cabin. She was out of it before he put her on the bed.

Chapter Seven

Nothing Fits

A clicking sound woke her and she tried to shut it out because her head hurt like someone was using it for a basketball. A groan escaped and she put her hand to her head. She was in bed. Cracking open her eyes, she saw blurry shapes. She rubbed them and tried again and her surroundings came into focus. It was a suite in a space ship. Much smaller than her own, maybe single deck. It had to be the main cabin. The clicking noise was coming from the desk. McDevitt was sitting there. Her handheld and what remained of her clothes were neatly stacked on the desktop. He was using his own handheld. From the sound of it, he was playing a game.

'Awake?' He sat forward, put down his handheld and reached for a cup. 'Drink this. It will help.'

She swiped at his hand but he saved the liquid from spilling. 'What did you do that for? It will help with the headache.'

Hands clenched to the side of her head, she screamed, then she let rip. 'How dare you drug me? By god you've a bloody nerve abducting me, pretending to be helping me. How could you? You. You! Bloody low life!'

There wasn't anything to throw at him, she found a pillow and tossed that. Again he defended his cup of medicine.

'It's not like that.'

'Isn't it?' She looked down at herself. She had a large white t-shirt over her underwear. 'You even removed my clothes. How dare you...you bloody pervert!'

He tilted his head sideways and grinned. 'There really wasn't much left of the dress and I sorta already saw all the rest, your underwear, I mean.'

Lowering her hands, she opened and closed her mouth like a big fish. Not even a splutter came to mind. Then she burst into tears.

'Ah now. Don't do that. Don't cry. That's just not on. There's a rule on this ship.'

Opi blubbered into her hands. 'Rule?'

'Yes, no crying.'

She cried louder. 'I feel like shiiiit,' she said in a drawn out sing song voice.

There was humour in his voice. 'I bet you do. Now look, take the drink. It will help. You won't feel like shit anymore and we can talk reasonably. Okay?'

'But you've abducted me.' She was still crying, knees drawn up face pressed to them.

He shrugged. 'Technically that is true, but it wasn't planned. Come on. Dry those tears. I did it to save your life.'

She lifted her head. He patted her face with a tissue.

'My life, my ass.'

He nodded and the grin grew wider. 'I saved your delectable ass too.'

She found the other pillow and hit him with it. With a raised elbow, he deflected it easily. 'Have you finished now? Drink it.'

'No.'

'Drink it now or I'll throw it out and won't offer you another one and you can keep your stinking headache.'

Her head thumped. She looked at him with narrowed eyes. 'Will it really help? You aren't sedating me again?'

'It's not a tranquilliser. It's a pain killer.' He held it out. She took it and looking away from him, took a sip, then another and then downed it.

He pulled out a drawer and rummaged through it. Curious, she turned her head to watch what he was doing. He held up some plain cotton trousers with a pull string waist and considered them, one hand rubbing his chin. 'Mmm...these ought to do it. I think they are Lucinda's.' He chucked them on the bed. He pulled out a bright pink t-shirt that had a picture of a white bunny with sparkly wings. That joined the trousers on the bed. 'Something for you to wear.' He stood up and shut the drawer with his foot. 'Ship's briefing in fifteen minutes. The san is in that cubicle there. It's small so you can only back in there, sorry.' He flapped his folded elbows like a chicken. 'No room to move.'

He left and the door shut behind him. The painkiller was working fast. She really did need to use the san. The unit was a tight fit. She wondered how he managed, being so much wider and taller. The toilet retracted into the wall and then the shower engaged. She pulled the pins out of her hair and washed it free of all the treatments that had been plastered on it. Then the dry cycle fluffed out her hair and made her feel like new.

The mirror revealed that the makeup Perri, the technician, had used was semi-permanent. Her eyes were still made up and her lips were undeniable red. Great.

The clothing was tight. She was a bit bigger than the fourteen year old daughter. It was hard to see, but she thought the trousers hugged her butt more than she was comfortable with. Made it look bigger. Groaning, she looked down at her bare feet and rolled her eyes. Now that she had had her rant, she didn't feel in danger. He'd saved her from a space pirate. Maybe he saved her from a whole bunch. It wasn't easy to trust anyone, particularly coming so close on the suspicion that one of her trusted inner circle had betrayed her. McDevitt appeared to be straight up. Yet, she was pretty sure he was up to something. What she didn't know.

The door opened when she stepped up to it. Outside was a small room. McDevitt was there, so was another man, a young man. 'This is Elroy Endersley, or Double E, to his friends. He's my co-pilot this trip and Farm manager of the rest of the time.'

'Hello, Mr Endersley.' McDevitt gestured to a vacant seat and she pulled herself into it. She bumped her upper arm and winced. The tracking device wound was painful. She gritted her teeth and tried to be patient. Who had arranged that appointment? Her regular doctor? Polly? Rani?

'We are clear of Space Station Beta C and through the jumpgate. Damage from enemy fire was minimal. We just have a few more dents in our shielding. We managed to dump your tracker, Opi, before we went through the jumpgate but it is possible they may work out who you were with and where I'm likely to take you.'

'Where's that?' she asked. 'Is there coffee?' She peered around the room looking for a food dispenser.

Double E popped up from his seat and pulled some coffee out of the wall, tossed it to her. It was a kind of tube that self-heated when the drinking tube was inserted into the container. She took a sip and sighed.

McDevitt watched her. 'The only safe place I know is Islay 2.'

'The potato planet?'

His body went stiff. 'What do you mean potato planet? I grow lots of things, including grain and I make single malt whisky. Award winning whisky, if you must know.'

'Sure. Okay.' She waved a hand, desperate for the coffee to kick in. Damn him for drugging her. 'It's a bit out on the rim isn't it? Reinforcements will be hard to come by. What are the coordinates?'

'Why do you want to know?' he asked sharply, head jerking up.

'Why don't you want to tell me? I'm free to leave aren't I?'

'That depends. We have to do a security risk assessment first. I have the data feeds from the space station. If you like you can help me go over them. Maybe we can find out what happened to your people during the attack.'

'Okay. I'm happy to do that.'

'Any idea who your traitor might be?' He asked, eyelids lowering as he studied her face.

'No. None. I have to have evidence before I accuse people. I presume you'll let me use my handheld.'

'Yes. Sure. Once we reach planet side. I've taken the power cell out of it for now.'

'You've got a lot of nerve. You interfering...jumped up...'

He held up a hand that halted her tirade. 'I must after all, deliver my date home safe and sound.'

Stunned for a moment, Opi covered her mouth and then smiled. 'So it was a date.'

'Best date ever.'

'Worst date ever invented in the history of mankind,' she countered.

He frowned. 'Surely there have been worse ones.'

'Maybe. I'd like to see the evidence.'

Chapter Eight

To the Potato Planet

The scenes of the restaurant from McDevitt's vid camera were sobering. They had trashed the place, blew most of the fittings to smithereens and started cutting through the walls. There was no sound to the feed, but the rage was evident. The space pirates were severely pissed. After seeing the footage, she had to agree with McDevitt, they had been looking for her. She thought about her fight with Mueller about security. She'd said no to the bodyguard and no to Polly being with her. Had she played into the pirates' hands or had she saved the bodyguard and her assistant, Polly?

The chaos in the docking bay where her ship was stationed was hard to decipher. Her ship had been totalled and the vidfeed from the corridor showed her captain and navigator got off ship in time. Polly and Rani and possibly Pravi were in a hotel somewhere probably getting laid. That left Mueller and the rest of the security team to be accounted for.

Mueller would have been at station security bullying the hell out of them as a matter of course. It was his MO. Riley though...where was he? Dead or on station? McDevitt keyed through a number of other feeds. 'Wait. Stop.' Opi let out a sigh of relief. Riley and his men were shooting at pirates not far from the docking level. That meant they hadn't gone up with the ship which was a great relief. That meant all her team were safe. That left most of them still suspected of betraying her. Maybe. She found it hard to accept.

'Couldn't it have been a system's leak. A hack that got into my schedule?'

McDevitt still studied the feeds. 'No. You forget the tracker. That could have been put in anytime. While you slept. You could have been drugged, or like you suspect, while having a routine medical. But that would require collusion with the person preparing your shot, if not the doctor. I suspect it was done on the ship while you were out cold. Who had access to you while you were in your cabin?'

'My assistant, Polly. My other assistant Rani. Pravi my new bodyguard. Mueller. Riley. Captain Graves, too, I suppose.'

He lifted a shoulder. 'Basically anyone then.'

She met his gaze and looked down. 'Yes. I think so.'

'Right. It won't be long before we land. Just another jumpgate.' He lifted away from the viewscreen and ran his fingers through his hair. 'There's something I should tell you before we land.'

She lifted her eyebrows. 'What?' Were the potatoes sentient? She tried hiding her smile at the thought.

'My daughter, Lucinda.'

'Yes?'

'She may react a bit strangely when she sees you?'

'Why? Oh, because I look like someone she knows?'

McDevitt considered her for a moment. 'Yes.' He reached out and touched her hair, which was now in its usual bob.

He opened his mouth to speak, then hesitated. With a slight shake of his head, he tried again. 'You mentioned when we were escaping that it was too soon. What did you mean by that?'

Opi pursed her mouth, wondering if she should speak. She considered him, what he'd done for her. 'This mission was to draw the space pirates out when I had everything in place. I wasn't expecting them to hit the station. Not such a brazen attack. I believe that trashes plan A.'

He lifted his chin, eyes serious as they studied her. 'How many plans do you have?'

'Enough.'

'Spill.'

She sighed. 'I think up to Plan E unless I think up another.'

Double E's voice came over the loud speaker. 'Prepare for jumpgate.'

'You better get in the webbing or strapped in.' He raised a finger and wagged it at her. 'No transmissions until I get you to the deadroom. Then we will see.'

'Okay.'

McDevitt turned and went to the cockpit.

***

Outside on the planet's surface, Opi breathed in the pure air and was caressed by a cool breeze. No need for smog filters.

McDevitt stood beside her. 'It's oxygen rich, slightly more than Earth. Nitrogen is plentiful. That's why it is great for growing things.' He hoisted a pack onto his shoulder. 'We have to walk it from here.' He studied her feet. 'You okay in those?'

She carried her red high heels in her hand. They were the only part of her own clothing that remained, all the rest being borrowed. Even her underwear had gone in the recycler. On her feet she wore some light weight espadrilles, barely a step up from slippers.

The landing site, it couldn't be called a space port, was surrounded on all sides by sweeping fields of golden grain. If she hadn't seen the buildings when they descended she would have thought the place uninhabited. She gazed around her and narrowed her eyelids, as she tried to work out how far and decided it was best to ask. 'How far is it? Don't you have ground transport?'

'It's about four clicks. I do have a ground transport but it is currently being used in agriculture. My horses are stabled on the other side of the home complex and,' he paused to look her up and down, 'I'm not sure you are up for horseback riding.'

'Horseback?' She jerked her head back. 'Expensive hobby.'

'Not on Islay 2. A necessity.'

So she followed McDevitt as he made his way to a well-worn path. Double E was staying behind to service the ship. Her body seemed heavier in the planet's gravity but it wasn't Earth standard. 'For a small planet you have reasonable gravity.'

'Hard core.' He glanced at her sideways.

'Figures. Terraformed?'

'Yes, it didn't need much. Grow the atmosphere a bit, balance the soil, add a bit of this and a bit of that.'

Opi nodded. As a business it was tidy, potentially lucrative, at least enough to sustain a small corporation or cooperative.

'Population?' she asked as she trudged behind him.

'At present, about two thousand. Mostly worker/settlers who have a share in the co-op.'

'So how did you acquire this planet?'

He sighed. 'I wondered when you'd ask that. My father was an explorer, back in the days when there were planets up for grabs. He bought it and I inherited it.'

'You weren't born here were you?'

He shook his head and chuckled. 'No. On Earth. Lucinda was born here though.'

After being in space less than a week she was feeling her muscles as she walked. Telling herself it was good for her soul, she strode along without complaint. McDevitt took long strides, which he adjusted to hers every now and then when he got too far ahead.

The track through the grain ended and ahead was about five acres of grazing pasture surrounding a large homestead. A well-marked path, laid with flat colourful stones, led to the rear of the homestead, which consisted of a number of out buildings to the front, or was that the back and to the sides. Ornamental plants and garden beds littered the property.

An orchard crowded along the path, complete with benches for sitting on, a number of fountains and statues and a gated compound.

'That's the kitchen garden.' McDevitt couldn't quite hide his pride. Then there was a large patio. They had just stepped onto it when the sound of running feet reached them. A young girl with brown hair and eyes, wearing a t-shirt and wraparound skirt waved to them as she jogged up. As she neared, her steps slowed. Opi watched her warily at first and then relaxed. This must be Lucinda. The girl staggered to a stop, hunched over, one hand to her mouth and the other pointing at Opi.

Opi lifted her head, straightened her shoulders and shot a glance at McDevitt.

'Not possible!' The girl near screeched and then ran at Opi, swamping her in an embrace. 'Mummy!' Wet sobbing sounds in her ear alerted her to something that McDevitt failed to mention. He sent her a wide-eyed stare, shook his head and pleaded silently.

'Honey,' he said quietly coming up behind his daughter. He stroked her back. 'This is Ms Opeia Gayens. A business associate.'

The sobs subsided into hiccups. The girl did not let up her hold. McDevitt repeated his introduction. The girl sniffed and bit by bit released her, first lessening the force of her hold and then pulling away slowly, reluctantly. 'But?'

Her gaze locked onto her father's, shot back to Opi and her eyes narrowed. 'It looks a lot, I mean, she looks a lot like my mother.'

'Yes,' he agreed. 'The resemblance is uncanny. But I can assure you it is not your mother.'

Lucinda edged back another step. Wiping her eyes, she looked Opi up and down, head shaking slightly. Opi smiled a little smile. Nervous. Embarrassed. Totally out of her depth. McDevitt had a lot of explaining to do. She could thump him for not telling her everything.

The girl let out a cry, covered her mouth and ran off, wailing loudly. A door slammed.

McDevitt's cheeks were red. He cleared his throat. 'I'm sorry about that. If you could make yourself at home in the lounge, I need to speak to my daughter. I fear she has suffered a bigger shock than I expected.'

'She's not the only one.'

He held the door open for her. 'There are drinks in the dispenser over there. Make yourself at home. I'll be back shortly.'

Then he was gone. Letting out a huge sigh, Opi surveyed the room. That was one odd encounter. Was the girl suffering from a mental illness or something? McDevitt did say she would have a strange reaction. From the dispenser she ordered up a spritzer drink strong on citrus and low on sugar. As she parsed the room, she was drawn to a photo sitting on a bookshelf by the large windows that overlooked a balcony and the mountains in the distance. A chair on the balcony looked like the one where McDevitt had recorded his message to her, his invitation. It wasn't quite sunset yet. A few hours more she suspected. She fingered a picture frame where photos paged from one to another. Picking it up she saw photos of a young girl in various stages of growth, she saw a photo of a woman holding a toddler who was learning to walk. The woman smiled up into the camera, eyes full of joy and love. The woman was her.

Chapter Nine

Double Trouble

Shakily, Opi put the photograph display down and backed away. Oh god, that was too scary to contemplate. It put a whole slant on McDevitt, him asking her out, him bringing her here. He'd married her clone. A clone she knew nothing about. She thought she knew the rest of them. Vee, damaged but rescued. Others ended before they knew life.

Opi forgot the spritz drink and ordered up something more potent. A lychee martini ought to achieve what she was going for. Her heart was heavy and her mind was overtaxed with all the subtle trickery that surrounded her. Could she trust no one? What crazy reason did McDevitt have for bringing her here?

Her mood was quite a deal more mellow by the time McDevitt returned. He took one look at her and said, 'You'd be wanting an explanation I expect.'

She levered herself out of the chair, sitting supported by her elbows. 'What kind of sick bastard are you? I was half-way to trusting you. But no, you're just like all the rest. You have an agenda. Never mind how I feel about it. What I want.'

He let out a sigh. 'What are you drinking?' He came over and sniffed it, a ghost of a smile on his face. 'I remember those. Powerful hangovers if you go one too many. Mind if I join you?' He walked to the dispenser. 'Another?'

When she lifted her glass she realised she had emptied it already. 'Yes. Damn it. I do.'

He brought the drink to her and passed it over. 'I didn't know. I didn't know until I met you. And you were so prettied up with your hair and makeup that I couldn't quite be sure. Couldn't pin you. I thought it was my mind playing tricks on me. Seeing her, seeing Belle.

'Then once you changed on the ship and I saw your hair and you were more relaxed, my doubts sort of fled. I didn't know how to tell you. I thought about telling you, thinking up scenarios but…'

Her gaze locked onto his, her sails so full of rage floundered. 'Are you telling me the truth?' she asked in an unsteady voice. Her emotions were ping ponging all over the place. With the rage gone, there was nothing there but horror and sorrow and fear.

'Yes. I never saw an up close shot of you. If you looked familiar in the shots I saw I didn't place you.'

'You realise you married a clone?' Her voice was unsteady. 'My clone?'

He turned toward the window, folding his arms with one hand rubbing his chin. It took a while for him to answer. 'I do now.'

She dropped the drink onto the side table in sort of a daze. All the confusion and lost feelings rose up inside. To her acute embarrassment she burst into tears.

A few moments later. She wasn't sure how long, he was beside her, enfolding her in his arms. 'I'm sorry it was such a shock. I should have given you more warning. By then we had no choice we had to come here.' He kissed the top of her head and stroked her back. Her crying fit subsided and she pushed away, wiping at stray tears. 'I'm sorry you had to witness that. I'm not normally so emotional. My life seems to be giving me a few kicks these days.' She met his gaze. 'Your poor daughter. Is she okay? What a shock for her. I take it you didn't know Belle was a clone.'

He shook his head. He stayed kneeling by her side, so close she could feel his heat, hear his breathing. 'Not while we were together,' he said softly. 'When she died the way she did, it was hinted at. Not confirmed mind you, just a theory. Our facilities here aren't that tech savvy.'

'Tell me. Did she have a good life? Was she happy?'

His eyebrows furrowed as his eyes tracked over her face. 'Yes, I believe she did have a good life. She was an easy going woman. This was home to her and she lived for her daughter and for me too. If that doesn't sound too conceited.'

She shook her head, fighting the need to cry again. She sniffed. 'I'm glad she was happy. I didn't know she existed. How did you meet?'

He sat back on his heels. 'I rescued her during one of my missions. She had nowhere to go to so we sort of drifted together. I'd just settled here and I brought her along, offered her land to build a home. Eventually we married.'

Opi nodded. 'I think I should contact my people now. You said you had a deadroom.'

He reached over to move a lock of hair from in front of her eyes. 'I know this is weird for you. I just want you to know that you're different from her. This isn't some weird...' He shrugged. 'I don't know what you would call it.'

He smiled, and his eyes sparkled. Opi's heart turned over. He was attractive and she had to be out of her mind not to notice. Yet, the business woman took control of the moment. 'The deadroom?' Opi just couldn't deal with the emotion soup right now. It was easier to perform Ms Gayens instead. She needed to get herself sorted. Initiate plan B and C and find out who her traitor was.

He studied her face for a moment, then tilted his head. 'Sure.' He got up and indicated with his hand for her to precede her through the door and into a corridor. Downstairs in a basement was a set of rooms. He opened the door to the one on the right and smiled her in. 'You can receive transmissions here on your handheld. Don't transmit anything. Not just yet. I'm hoping you will share any intel.'

He checked her over. 'You left your shoes in the lounge. I'll put them in your room for you. Clothes...I'll see what I can dig up. For now, go ahead.' He dug out her power cell and handed it over.

Her handheld jumped to life once she reinserted the power cell and put her thumb to the reader. There were a number of messages. 'On screen.'

The feed switched to McDevitt's wall screen. Noise assaulted her ears. Cries, commands, sirens. Polly filled the screen. 'Opeia? Opi? Where are you damn it? Did you run off with McDevitt? The ship was blown up. We lost the navigator. The rest of us are okay. Come in.' She looked to the side. 'I don't know,' she yelled impatiently to someone out of shot. Then leaning in, she said urgently. 'Opeia you must get in contact with us. With me. Let me know where you are. How you're doing.'

Opi's pulse quickened and she itched to contact her assistant. The next message in the queue was Mueller. He wore a bandage around his neck barely disguising a weapons' burn. 'Ms Gayens. We were sabotaged. It was an inside job. Someone on the station overloaded the internal spin generator that threw the gravity into chaos. They knew where you were, knew where your ship was docked. Please contact me. If you are with McDevitt then you have a chance. Don't trust anyone else. Even me. We are compro...' The message cut out.

'Interesting,' McDevitt was back.

'Were you eavesdropping on both those calls?' she flashed him a hot look.

'Yes. I was standing here by the door. You just didn't notice. So Mueller says they are compromised.'

'Did he? I didn't quite catch the end.'

'It was pretty clear. That means either your people can't be trusted or they are captives of the space pirates and anything they say or do is suspect. Understand?'

She narrowed her gaze. 'Yes. Goddamn it all to hell. Those bastards.'

He tilted his head. 'My thoughts exactly. I suggest no transmissions.'

'But surely in this deadroom I can let them know I'm all right. It won't be traced.'

He studied her and his gaze flicked back to the screen. 'Scan the rest of your messages and then we'll talk.'

He turned and left. Opi stared at her handheld. He may not want her to contact her people but she could initiate plan B and C. Like McDevitt said, it wouldn't take them long to work out where she went and with who. She needed to be prepared.

On leaving the deadroom, she went in search of McDevitt. A terrible thought occurred to her. If they did track her here with him then the battle was going to be here. Not the place of her choosing. Damn them all to hell.

The scent of smoke drew her to the patio where McDevitt was cooking slices of meat on a grill. He waved an implement in her direction. 'Hungry? I thought we'd have some Islay 2 hospitality. Home grown beef.' He gave his barbeque a healthful prod with his oversized fork. 'Roast potatoes and salad coming up.'

When she didn't respond he glanced up at her. 'What is it?'

She pursed her lips and rubbed her upper arms against the cooling breeze. The sun was going down and night brought a touch of ice on the wind. 'Do your people have bunkers? Somewhere they can take cover?'

He studied her for a moment and looked back down at the food. 'If I sound the alarm they can find cover.'

Tears burned her eyes. 'I don't want...want anyone getting hurt. It wasn't what I bargained for.'

'Just you you mean. You're prepared to face them, to die?'

She nodded, finding it hard all of a sudden to keep her emotions in. He had a daughter. A daughter that was half hers genetically. Why had she said yes to that damn dinner date? It was all her fault.

'I have Double E monitoring the space around here. We'll have time. In the meantime, pull up a chair. Lucinda is bringing in the salads.'

Her head jerked up at her words. He came over, put his arm around her shoulders and squeezed. 'I've talked to her. She's okay. It was the surprise more than anything. She wasn't around when Belle died.'

'You explained about clones to her?'

'Pretty much. I said it was like her mother was your twin sister. A completely separate person, although you share the same DNA.'

Opi nodded. 'Thank you.' Bolstered, she was prepared as she could be to sit down with her new niece.

The girl had dark shadows under her eyes. Her smile was faint when she brought in the bowls of salad and placed them on the table. She walked back into the house and came back a few minutes later with a basket of bread and a tray of roast potatoes just as McDevitt slid a huge steak onto Opi's plate.

It looked and smelled delicious, but the worry in her gut ruined her appetite.

McDevitt sat down opposite her and Lucinda too the end of the table so she was sitting next to both of them. 'I'm...' Lucinda began. 'I'm sorry I got upset before. It was the surprise.'

Opi speared a piece of cucumber and sent her a shy smile. 'I'm sure it was a huge shock. There was no way to prepare you. I'm sorry. I didn't know before...you understand.'

'Dad explained it.' She flicked her gaze to her father. 'He loved my mother a lot.'

Opi's heart squeezed. Belle had scored better in those stakes than she had herself. But there was no point in envying someone else's life. Hers was set out before her and she had a job to do.

'Do you go to school here?' she asked Lucinda.

'No. I go to school on Earth, but I'm on long vacation.'

'Do you like it on Earth?'

Lucinda cocked her head to the side as she studied Opi, perhaps looking for the nuances of her mother's face. 'It's okay. A bit crowded, but I am studying agricultural science and economics. In a year I'll be able to finish my course from here. On the farms I can do all my practical assignments.'

Opi smiled at her enthusiasm. 'I'm happy for you. I'm sure your father will be pleased you will join him in the business.'

Lucinda shook her head. 'It's not a business, it's a lifestyle. Earth is on its last legs. This is the future.'

'Right.' Opi sliced off some steak and put it in her mouth. It was soft and flavoursome and she chewed it with relish. The girl wasn't too wrong if the predictions she'd been hearing were accurate.

McDevitt lifted a gravy boat. 'Sauce? This is mushroom and garlic.'

Still eating she nodded and he poured the sauce all over her steak. He chucked on some potatoes. 'You have to try those. Our potatoes are the most flavoursome ever. Something in the soil here gives them the edge over any other. Soon people will be recommending Islay potatoes.'

She swallowed. Her spirit lifting as her appetite improved. 'I'll try some.'

He filled her glass with a bright red wine. 'Local?'

He shook his head. 'Imported.' He checked the label. 'Australian. I am useless at making wine. We have some vineyards here but we sell the grapes to off planet vintners.'

So as the sun set over Islay 2, painting the heavens with ribbons of red and yellow and orange, Opi ate barbeque steak and chatted and laughed all the while fearing that this was the calm before the storm, a moment to be held and cherished before it disappeared forever.

They all helped clear up, placing the crockery and utensils in the washer and the leftover meat in the refrigerator.

Lucinda wished her good night with a smile and gave her father hug and a kiss. McDevitt watched her with love in his eyes. That look warmed the cockles of Opi's heart. Her daughter had not received a father's love, rather his ire.

'Good night,' she said and turned away.

He grabbed her hand. 'Wait. Not yet.'

Her heart skipped a beat. Why was she so conscious of him? It totally wasn't going to work out. They could not have a thing. She could not have a thing with her clone's husband and he couldn't have anything with her. It was sick. It was—

Her thought was cut off when his lips met hers. Tentative at first, his kiss grew bold, more demanding. Her hands squeezed his shoulders and they were a solid as they looked. His arms came around and he drew her closer and she closed her eyes, surrendering to the moment. Then he eased off and pushed her gently back.

His blue eyes were bright in the kitchen light as he studied her. 'I'm sorry,' he shrugged. 'I'm not sure what came over me.'

Opi wasn't expecting to hear that. She thought perhaps it would be 'will you sleep with me tonight' or 'care to walk in the light of the moons' but no it was an apology.

'Um…well…okay…don't do it again. Good night.' Her face heated and she blindly stumbled to the room he had allocated her. This could not be made right. She let him kiss her. She'd participated. She had advertised that she was attracted to him. It was all her own fault.

After a shower where she donned a borrowed nightie that barely covered her generous behind, she slid into bed. Punching the pillows helped to settle her.

Damn it! Damn him!

Chapter Ten

Horses for Courses

Opi sipped her second cup of coffee while she stood in front of the large picture windows and watched the cloud shadows glide over the mountains in the distance. It was so peaceful here. A trifle unnerving. On Earth where she lived and worked, there was noise and people twenty four hours a day. And pollution and climate instability. This pristine world was unexpected. Here she could place no more than four people in close proximity. Looking down at her clothes she decided this was a good thing. She wore bright pink track pants that were two sizes too small and a purple t-shirt with the words "I'm a princess" printed across her breasts. The t-shirt was also a tad tight. Yet beggars can't be choosers. She might have to opt for borrowing McDevitt's clothes. They, at least, would hide some of her bodily sins.

Wind rippled the grain in the fields below, sending patterns of dark gold to tease her eye. A sound behind alerted her to someone entering and she turned around. 'Good morning,' she said to Lucinda. Now that they had sorted themselves out, Lucinda and Opi were able to dance around each other with more ease.

'Good morning to you, too,' Lucinda replied as she came in and helped herself to fresh orange juice, that someone, possibly McDevitt had prepared. A large bowl of oranges sat on the counter. Opi was tempted but she needed the coffee to get her system functional. So far it wasn't working. Her old buddy caffeine was letting her down.

Lucinda came to stand up beside her, taking a sip of her juice. After swallowing a few mouthfuls she said, 'Do you like the view?'

Opi smiled. 'Yes, very much. And you, do you like this place?'

'I do. I've been on station a couple of times, but it smells there. Stale, oily like machinery and like there's no sun, which there isn't, of course. I like it here best of all.'

'You go to school on Earth though?'

'Yes, Dad insists but I don't like it there. Don't tell him I said so though. He thinks he's doing the right thing.'

'What's wrong with Earth?'

Lucinda met her eye for eye. 'There is too much pollution, too many people and so much rage.'

'Rage? What do you mean?'

Lucinda lowered her gaze and played with her glass. 'Well on the streets, on the news broadcasts, on the social media streams. All of it is spewing rage about something.'

Opi narrowed her gaze and nodded. 'I'd not thought of it that way. I guess I insulate myself from that much exposure to it. I know it's there but I don't engage.'

Lucinda put her glass away in the washer and then stood up. 'Would you like to go on a picnic today?'

'A picnic?'

'Yes, there is a small green wood not far from here. It has a lovely stream and a waterfall. It would be great and I'd love to show it to you.' Lucinda studied Opi's expression. 'You do know what a picnic is?'

A heavy tread by the door announced the arrival of McDevitt into the conversation. 'I wouldn't bet that Ms Gayens does know what a picnic is, Lu.'

Opi strode away from the window and placed her coffee cup in the washer. 'I do know what a picnic is actually.' She frowned as she took a plate and studied the abundance of food on offer. She really shouldn't eat hash browns, they go straight to her butt. She forked two onto her plate. 'I just can't recall being on one. Not since I was like six years old.'

McDevitt harrumphed and Lucinda exclaimed. 'Not since you were six? That's crazy. Didn't you take your daughters on picnics?'

Opi scooped some mushrooms onto her plate. 'No. At least I don't remember doing so.'

Lucinda was obviously appalled at this lack of proper entertainment for Opi's daughters. 'No picnics? No, that's not possible.'

Opi looked up from choosing between fried and scrambled eggs. 'You may be surprised at the cultural poverty of my life.'

Lucinda went to her father and laid a hand on his forearm. 'Come on, dad. Convince Ms Gayens to come on a picnic with us.'

He laughed. 'Oh so I'm invited on this excursion of yours.'

'Of course, we need you to prepare the food.'

'Mercenary child.'

Lucinda moved away to take a seat at the table. Opi sat down opposite her. 'So will you? Come on both of you. It's an amazing day. There's hardly any wind.'

'I am game if you are,' McDevitt said to her.

Opi looked around her. There wasn't much else to do. She wasn't used to being so idle and it wasn't like she was going to be here forever or that she'd ever come back again to have a second chance at a picnic in the wood with a stream and a waterfall. 'Sure. I'm game.'

***

'What do you mean we are riding horses?' Opi was standing stiff as a board, trying to adjust to the size of the animal that Lucinda was placing a saddle on. It stomped huge feet and tried to nip at Lucinda as she ducked to tie straps under its big round belly.

'It's the only way to get there. It's too far to walk. Don't tell me you've never ridden a horse?'

'Of course I haven't. They are rare on earth. I haven't been this close to one in my life. Good god, did that horse just take a dump?'

Lucinda laughed. 'Of course, Terry will clean it up later and put it in the garden. He helps around the yard and horse manure makes for great vegetables.'

Opi put a hand on her stomach, which had decided to loop de loop. 'You put horse shit on the vegetables I take it. The ones I ate?'

'Yep. Chicken pooh too.'

McDevitt strode into the yard leading an even taller horse, with fine boned legs and a slashing tail of black hair. Lucinda looked up. 'Opi doesn't want to ride.'

McDevitt cast her a glance then to the horse Lucinda was saddling. 'Really? I can't believe that.' He tied his horse to a pole and strode over. 'I've seen you in action Opi. If you can manage access chutes in a space station with fluctuating gravity you can manage a horse.'

Opi lifted her chin, trying to ignore the backhanded compliment. 'That wasn't by choice, I'll have you know.'

McDevitt strode up to her. 'You're not scared are you? I could carry you in my arms.' He waggled his eyebrows.

Opi lowered her head and glared. 'Scared?'

McDevitt hummed and ran a hand down the mare's nose. 'Miss Muffett is so quiet she's practically dead. You just have to sit on her and she'll follow us.'

Opi tried to avoid his eye. McDevitt nodded. 'Oh, I see how it is.'

He tapped Lucinda on the shoulder. 'Let me finish that. You saddle up, Starkiller.'

Opi's eyes widened as McDevitt led Miss Muffett over to her. The animal seemed so huge. 'You wouldn't want to disappoint my daughter would you?'

Opi flicked her gaze up to meet his. The blue of his eyes seemed paler in the sunlight. 'I didn't know there'd be horses.'

He grinned, looked back at the horse and then tied its reins to a post. 'You run board meetings, take over companies, and jet all over the sector in spiffy space ships. You take on space pirates and rattle your sword. You can ride this horse, guaranteed.'

Her eyes surveyed the horse. 'I don't know. I'm terrified.'

McDevitt's hand touched her upper arm. 'I thought you were terrified of me, yet you gentled.'

She swiped his hand off her arm. 'I was never terrified of you. Don't be ridiculous. Besides I'm not a horse. I'm definitely not gentled.'

'Okay then. Put your left foot in the stirrup there and I'll boost you up. Then just sit there quietly while we get the rest of the gear ready.'

Opi supressed a moan. 'I can't.'

'You can. Put your hand on my shoulder. Now put your foot here. That's right. Now I'm going to lift you but you need to swing the other leg up over and stick your foot into the stirrup on the other side.'

Opi sat on the horse. It was so high she was sure if she looked down that she'd fall flat on her face. McDevitt gave her swift and precise instructions about how to balance, turn the horse, point her toes and get the horse going. 'Don't worry if she doesn't move on her own. She'll walk when we start.'

Before she could frame an eloquent riposte, Lucinda walked a caramel coloured horse out. It had a white star between its eyes. Starkiller's steps were prancing and he shook his mane and jerked his head about.

McDevitt packed the saddle bags with their picnic supplies. 'What's your horse called?' she asked him.

'Roo, on account of him jumping around a lot when he was just a foal.'

'Roo? You mean like in Kangaroo?'

'Yes, but his real name is Demon King. That's what is on his registration, but we just call him Roo.'

'Miss Muffett?' she asked.

'That's her name. Placid thing. Nothing bothers her as long as she eats.'

Lucinda finished saddling her horse and climbed on board. With her nod to her father, he said, 'Right then. Let's go.' McDevitt swung up onto his horse. Roo danced and pranced, make a show of tossing its head, then McDevitt controlled him and nudged on. Starkiller glided out the gate and Miss Muffett plodded along behind.

***

The clip clop sound of the horses sounded over loud as they followed the path through the hushed woodland. Filtered light bathed the surroundings. Strange smells tantalised her. Leaves of all shapes and sizes on the trees and on low ferns drew her eye. She'd never seen up close before. The outer rim of the woodland had looked to be a plantation but the inner woods looked natural to her eye. The deeper they went in, the dimmer the sunlight became muted through the thick canopy overhead.

'What do you think?' McDevitt asked her.

'It's lovely. I'm impressed.' Opi was surprised by her reaction to the woodland, to sitting on an animal and to McDevitt's space. Her surroundings soothed her on a level she didn't really comprehend. It distanced her from her worries, from the life she led. Concerns drifted away.

'How are you going on the horse? Okay?'

Opi smiled as she met his gaze. 'Yes, fine. Although, it does feel interesting in a certain place.' Her bottom was getting a fine massage and her legs were kind of numb.

On their way to the picnic spot, Lucinda had taken off on a gallop down the lane and then raced back again. She said she wanted to shake the fidgets out of her horse. As she'd sought her father's permission, Opi had to keep her protest to her herself. The thought of the young girl charging off on a wild animal had her maternal instincts firing off and she barely kept her mouth shut, barely clamped them down. *Not your daughter, Opi.*

Miss Muffett had only shifted sideways when Starkiller took off. McDevitt kept control over his mount. Roo wanted to stretch his legs also. It sidestepped and tossed its head. McDevitt slapped its neck and talked to it.

'You can join her if you like,' Opi said to be polite. She didn't actually want to be left alone on the strange beast.

McDevitt grimaced. 'No. I'm happy here taking it slowly.'

Opi appreciated McDevitt staying with her. Being thrown off a horse was not on her bucket list.

Farther in, they followed a winding path down. McDevitt fired some more instructions off to her. Opi wanted to get off and walk on her own two feet, but held on and leant back as advised. At the bottom of the ravine was a large pool which fed a stream. Looking up, she saw water pouring over rocks above.

On the shores of the pool they halted. A wide green flat patch of grass appeared to be their picnic spot. 'What do you think, Opi?' Lucinda asked as she dismounted.

As Opi was gazing at the ground and was trying to gauge how far away it was, she didn't answer. McDevitt came over. 'Here, let me help you down. Lucinda hold Miss Muffett.'

'Oh sorry.' The girl darted over.

With Lucinda holding the reins, Opi followed McDevitt's instructions on how to dismount and he steadied her. 'Oh that's an interesting sensation. I don't think my legs work anymore.'

Lucinda took Miss Muffett to drink and then over to where the other horses were tethered. McDevitt sized her up. 'I think walking around…gently will help ease the kinks. Don't fall in.' He walked over to his horse and opened the saddle bags. 'I'll get the picnic ready.'

McDevitt was right. After walking around for a bit and easing her back, she did feel better and was able to enjoy the surrounding. The waterfall had to be at least twenty metres high, a gently flowing thing that added its music to the forest sounds. Soft waves of branches, the various calls of birds and the sounds of their party held her in thrall. She turned and watched McDevitt and Lucinda work together, chatting amiably as they laid out a blanket and food on the soft grass. It touched Opi's heart. It was a simple thing, yet what pleasure it brought.

Before she made a fool herself and started blubbering she threw her head back and looked up at the canopy. Why was she being such an idiot? Because malekind was redeeming itself in her eyes? No, she was never so stupid as to think all men were evil and abusive as her husband had been. Her daughters had nice men in their lives after all. But as she sent her gaze back and caught Lucinda waving and calling to her, she knew regret. Regret that her daughters hadn't had this. That she hadn't had this.

While the absence of work left her feeling bereft of purpose, she found the peaceful surroundings and company gently easing away her tension.

Opi took her place next to Lucinda on the blanket and accepted a fresh hunk of bread spread with butter. 'Thank you.'

McDevitt tilted his head and said, 'Are you all right?'

Opi put up a smile. 'Perfectly. Thank you. Now is that chicken I see over there?'

He smiled and held out the wrapper which contained slices of white meat. 'Tea?' he asked raising a flask up.

'Thank you, I will.'

And so Opi enjoyed her first horse ride, her first picnic on the planet of Islay 2, with Owain McDevitt and his daughter, Lucinda. If she did feel a touch emotional, she decided it was warranted. Another quick glance at McDevitt and she noticed the intensity of his gaze. It made her heart skip a beat.

After the meal was packed up, Lucinda bounced to her feet. 'I'm going to climb up. Watch for me.'

Opi floundered. 'Climb up what?'

Lucinda gave her father a peck on the cheek, then pointed to the top of the waterfall. 'Up there. Don't worry I don't expect you to come.' She ran off, just like that.

Opi turned to McDevitt. 'Are you sure it's safe?'

He lay across the blanket supporting himself with his elbow, hand propping up his head. 'She loves that climb and has done it many times. Relax. Come here and stretch out. There's plenty of room.'

Her eyebrows furrowed. 'Why?'

'Because that's what you do at a picnic. You eat and then you lie down and rest.'

'Oh? I see.' Opi considered this, uncurled her legs and slid over closer to McDevitt. He lay diagonally across the blanket, which meant she had to as well if she wanted to stretch out. Aligning herself to his body, she asked, 'Is this what you mean?'

'Yes, perfect.'

He stretched out his arm. 'Here, use this as a pillow.'

Opi pushed up, glanced from him to the arm. 'Won't I hurt you?'

He laughed. 'How heavy is your head?'

She pursed her lips and nodded. 'Okay. You asked for it.'

Tentatively, she laid her head on his arm. He adjusted himself so that he lay closer to her and his other arm came over her waist.

'What are you doing?' she asked quietly.

'Cuddling you.'

'That's not part of the picnic is it?'

'Mmm,' he replied sleepily.

Opi lay there listening and after a few minutes his breathing changed. He had fallen asleep it seemed. Lucinda didn't call out and so Opi's eyelids started to lower too as she also fell asleep.

The sound of twigs breaking woke her. She sat up with a snort and wiped her mouth. She cringed. Had she drooled on McDevitt's arm?

Looking around, she saw Lucinda at the horses, tightening straps. 'Oh you're back.' Opi stretched and sloughed of her residual fatigue. 'Must have fallen asleep. How was it?'

Lucinda came over. Her dad made waking noises. 'I saw you two from the top,' Lucinda commented, a sly grin on her face. 'Fast asleep. It looked kind of cute.'

'Oh?' Opi shot McDevitt a sour look. 'Your dad said people sleep after eating at a picnic.'

Lucinda's eyes leapt to her father's. 'Oh yeah, they do. Particularly the oldies.'

McDevitt leaped up and tousled Lucinda's hair. 'Who are you calling oldie?' The pair giggled as they darted about and then they packed up.

***

Her aching butt and throbbing thighs kept her awake for many hours that night. Even with the bath that McDevitt suggested she take to soothe her muscles, the pain was sufficient for her to need pain relief. Once she'd taken that she slid into sleep, until she woke suddenly.

It was so quiet and dark when Opi opened her eyes that she was disoriented. Try as she might she couldn't go back to sleep. Her mind was full. Emotions roiled beneath the surface. Emotions she hadn't had to deal with for a long time. A crack in the surface of her heart maybe, that leaked need and want and desire? Until then, she didn't realise she'd been so closed off. It had been cosy with McDevitt at the picnic. It had felt nice to lie there with him. Just to be there. Not doing anything at all.

Yet, it was all screwed up. McDevitt had loved and married her clone. What must it be doing to him having her here in this house that he shared with her? It was doing her head in every time the thought cropped up. She had to admit that often she forgot about the clone for short periods of time at least.

Sitting up, she pushed the hair out of her eyes. It must be doing his head in. It was certainly bending hers out of shape. She could not be attracted to her clone's widower. It was not politically correct. More than that their lives were incompatible. He was a farmer. She was head of AllEarth Corp. But that was long term thinking. She didn't need long term thinking. She needed to be in the now.

Tossing off the bed covers, she slipped out of bed and then out of the room. There were dim lights down low that illuminated the corridor and she was able to find her way outside onto the patio. A hush lay over the land along with a fine tendril of mist. The wind was absent and birds were calling to each other. Sunrise was not far away.

A movement alerted her that she was not alone outside. Looking down into the carefully lit garden below she saw a shape—a man moving, kicking, punching, blocking in a precise form. By the size of him, it was McDevitt. He wore nothing but tight-fitting black shorts that clung to his thighs until just above the knees. In the low-powered lighting, Opi watched McDevitt perform his kata and enjoyed the view—controlled movement and muscles sliding fluidly under skin. With a sigh, she moved away, conscious of being found staring.

If she was up this early it was worth catching the sunrise. The mountains were dark and that was where the sun set. The sun must come up on the other side so she found the corridor that led to the exit to the back garden.

The door opened as she approached. Sensors, she suspected. Stepping through, it snapped shut behind her. This garden was full with the scent of flowers, dark shadowed paths, and the blurred shapes of ponds and small fountains. She followed along the most direct route, her eyes on the horizon that was kissed with gold light, growing brighter with each breath that she took. Then she reached the edge, a small rise in the land that provided a view of the fields beyond.

The sun was small and bright and Opi let out a sigh. What a pretty place this was. She couldn't remember the last time she'd had time to watch the sunrise. If she'd been awake she had barely noticed.

The sound of a step behind her warned her of someone approaching. 'You're up early.'

With a smile, she returned McDevitt's greeting, keeping her eye on the horizon. 'Yes. I woke up and couldn't get back to sleep.'

He chuckled. 'Me too. Strange that.' He came to stand beside her. Her gaze slanted sideways and she sucked in breath. He was bare-chested, a thin towel around his neck. She hadn't expected this. Naked flesh. He loomed beside her and she had to drag her gaze away and back to the sunrise. 'It's beautiful,' she said as the sun blazed fully over the horizon. She had to shade her eyes.

Turning toward him, she looked up into his face, disturbed to find him staring at her and not the view. 'What's wrong?'

He shook his head, put his hands on her shoulders. 'I have to confess, Opi, this is driving me crazy.'

'What?'

'This.'

He drew her closer, lowered his head and caught her mouth in a teasing, light kiss. Like he was tasting her, sampling her. Opi tasted him back. Reckless, her mind told her, but she kept on. His lips were cool, but his mouth was hot. He broke off the kiss and nibbled her neck just below her right ear. She gasped at the contact and then he was back, lips on hers, tongue firm and sure, deepening the kiss so that it became a wrestling match, who was more passionate, more sunk into the moment. Rational thought was a bit difficult to locate and she gave up trying and just went with the sensation of being kissed and kissing.

His hands had wrapped tight around her, then lowered grabbing a handful of her butt.

'I love your body. So voluptuous.'

'You do?' Her brow crinkled and then she smiled. 'That's great.' Her hands were exploring his skin, the muscles twitching under her touch. 'I like your body too. So firm. So hot to the touch.'

Breathing hard, he caressed her, running his hands up her back. Her nightgown lifted and she realised with a shock that it was all she had on. He noticed too. Breaking the kiss he growled. 'Jesus. We can't do this here.'

'Do what?' Opi gaped at him.

He picked her up. 'My room is closer.'

Opi clung to him as he jogged into the house. Had she just consented to sex? Her heart thumped. It had been so long. Spikes of fear lanced into her body. She was no longer a young woman. What if she was no good? What if she forgot what to do?

A door slid open and McDevitt stood her on her feet. Not giving her a chance to protest his hungry mouth was on hers again. She backed up. He followed until she was pressed against the wall. Her hands ran all over his shoulders, his arms and his back. Then she grabbed handfuls of his firm ass and pressed herself to him. Her knees went weak and she surprised herself by groaning. Maybe it came naturally.

McDevitt pulled away. 'This will not do.'

He grabbed the collar of her nightgown and tugged. It split down the middle. Eyes wide she gaped at him. 'Why did you do that?'

There was a fire in his eyes as they roamed over her body followed closely by his hands, then his mouth. 'Beautiful.' Then giving her a peck on the chin, he added, 'Been a fantasy of mine forever.'

Tears stung her eyes. This was too real, too sudden. He noticed them and touched her face tenderly. Then leant in and kissed her softly. 'We can stop if you want.'

Time seemed to freeze as she studied his face, considered her own heart and mind. This might be her only chance—her one chance to get laid. 'I don't want you to stop.'

Her gaze lowered and she could tell he didn't want to either. But she was so pleased he offered her that choice. Lurching forward on her tip toes, she plastered her mouth over his. Two seconds later, they fell on the bed naked, McDevitt exploring her body with his hot, eager mouth while Opi prayed that the room had adequate sound proofing.

***

Opi woke up some time later. The window covering was mid-way open, letting in the blinding light of day. Her body ached pleasantly, well and truly used. McDevitt had been so gentle with her, particularly when she told him how long it had actually been since she'd had a sex partner. He had exclaimed rather bitterly that it was a tragedy and a waste and she'd giggled like a girl.

McDevitt had shown her things she'd not known before. How could she be forty two and not know about her clitoris? Now he had introduced her to it, she wanted more and more of him, of sex. If she didn't need to use the bathroom, she would have stayed in bed until he came back so they could start again.

But no. Business was bound to intrude. She felt it in her bones.

Thoughts that he wasn't in love with her but with her clone surfaced but she punched them back down. There was no point in wallowing. Best foot forward. He never spoke of love and what did she know about it anyway? McDevitt had placed a robe at the end of the bed. She slipped it on. On the chair was a folded pile of clothes. He'd left them for her. She checked them and shook her head. Purple track pants, white t-shirt with a bright daisy on it. She checked the fabric, it looked too thin.

Showered and dressed, Opi made her way to the kitchen. Food was spread out. There was no sign of anyone so she picked up a plate and filled it with egg, bacon, mushrooms, hash browns and toast. As her coffee cup filled, she inhaled the aroma, eyes closing in appreciation. Did he grow the beans here? Made sense if he did. It was the best coffee she'd ever tasted and she'd tasted the best Earth had to offer. She was hungrier than she had felt in ages. It was amazing what sex could do for the appetite.

A smile lit her face as she parked herself on the patio and started in on her breakfast. Reclining in her seat, sipping coffee, she was alerted to the sound of someone running.

She got up from the table as McDevitt approached. All her senses on alert—something was wrong. He had a scowl on his face and his body signalled repressed anger, tight fists, legs pumping as they approached her. The body suit he wore only emphasised his physique. 'You lied to me,' he shouted as he approached.

She backed up. 'About what?'

He kept coming at her. He was an unexploded bomb. She backed away, but he grabbed her, held her chin in his hands, his face pressed close to hers. 'You're bloody transmitting. You've betrayed us all.'

Her brows furrowed. 'You're hurting me.'

He glared down into her face. 'I trusted you.'

'I trusted you!' she shouted back. If he had stabbed her in the gut he could not have wounded her more. 'I'm not transmitting. Let me go!'

He eased up his hold, blinking as he was only just aware how he held her. Shifting his grip, he clasped her shoulders. 'Double E says there's a tracking blip broadcasting from here. Where is it? The transmitter! Tell me.' His face was red and full of rage. Opi wondered at it. His voice had been so soft not a few hours before, his touch smooth and mellow.

Opi knew how to protect herself. Now her shock at his actions was past, she ground out. 'Let me go or I'll hurt you.'

His sneered at her. 'Like you could.'

Opi moved. He was bigger and stronger, but she had her moves. She grabbed his hand twisted and held. Now it was he who was gasping. 'I am not transmitting anything.' She spoke clearly and slowly so he would understand, over his painful breaths. 'My handheld is in your deadroom. I've got nothing of my own here except...'

She let him go. 'No!' she said in a voice that had sunk to the lowest depths.

'What?' he said quietly, assessing her with that bright gaze of his. Anger had washed away. His eyes focussed as the thought struck home.

'The shoes,' they said in unison.

McDevitt moved first and Opi ran after him. She came through the door as he was picking up the shoes. He turned them inspecting the heels. He twisted the heel cap and pulled out a small transmitter.

Opi doubled over. 'Polly! Oh god, no. Polly.'

'Your assistant?' McDevitt loomed. He brushed his hair off his face. 'I'm sorry.' He voice was soft, sympathetic.

'How could she?' Tears fell unchecked. Tears of rage, of betrayal, of hurt. Today was kicking her in the gut. First McDevitt now this. 'We were friends.'

He knelt down beside her where she was hunched over, hands protectively over her stomach. 'I know it kicks. But you don't know what they had over her. Maybe they had her family captive. Threatened to hurt someone. Everyone has a breaking point.'

She snapped at him. 'Shut up! You don't know anything!' She hit her chest, twice, two sharp thrusts. 'She was with me for years. She bought that whole stupid outfit for that ridiculous date.' Opi broke down then, collapsing onto the floor, abandoning herself to her self-pity.

'You looked great. She did a great job.'

Opi howled. 'She was my friend.'

'I know. I'm sorry.'

Opi didn't have the breath left inside her to form a reply.

After hovering around her for a few minutes, he stood up. 'Come to the command room when you're done. Maybe wash your face. You'll feel better then.' Then he left her alone.

Opi bawled her eyes out. Betrayal always hurt, but somewhere along the line she'd grown fond of Polly. Images of their time together replayed with bitter shame and hurt. It hadn't been real. Polly had played her. When was it going to stop? Only when she was dead or had nothing left to give. When she had nothing that anybody wanted.

'Opi?' She thought he'd left her alone with her misery.

Shame and anger stepped up to take control of her tongue. 'Bastard! Just leave me alone.'

'Okay then.'

The door snapped shut behind him and she was alone. It was her own fault. She was older, experienced, she should've known better. She'd rolled over and shown her soft belly, begged to be knifed in the gut. First with her team, with Polly and now McDevitt. She sobbed hard, raged at the ceiling, at her own stupidity. Didn't Carl's betrayal teach her anything? She was in the depths of despair.

Even McDevitt had turned on her. They'd had sex. So what? They didn't have a relationship just a silly rapport that meant nothing. How the hell could she be so stupid? Now, wasn't the time to be vulnerable. It was time to be tough.

In the scattered debris of betrayal, she found her heart and locked it up tight. She could do this. Control herself; face the foe. There was a battle to be fought, to be won. She'd lost sight of that like some adolescent. One hint of kindness, of sexual attraction and she'd fallen like the fool that she was. By god, she wished this wasn't her life.

In the bathroom she washed away the remnants of her hot tears with cool water. As she studied her complexion her mind ordered itself. Emotion was pushed back down, put under lock and key. If Polly had betrayed her, then she probably didn't act alone. All her team were suspect. Tears began in her eyes again. Eyes sore from weeping, further tears stung in irritation.

'No. Stop it. You don't shed a tear for them. They didn't spare a thought for you.'

Tidying her hair, she lifted her chin to study her reflection. 'You're Opeia Gayens, head of AllEarth Corp. Powerful, smart and deadly. You have a job to do. Stop moaning about your problems and grow some backbone.'

Turning on her heel, she left the bathroom and headed for the command room. She bumped into Lucinda.

The girl gave her a shy smile. 'Hi. Did you sleep okay? I hope you aren't too sore from the ride.' Lucinda gaped at her. 'Are you all right? Have you been crying?'

Opi kept her expression neutral. 'Good morning. I slept well, thank you. Could you direct me to the command room?'

'Oh sure. It's the deadroom just expanded. You know where that is right? Are you sure you're okay? Do you need to talk?'

Opi experienced the girl's kindness like the twist of a knife. Working hard to keep her expression neutral, she said, 'I'm fine. Thank you.' The smile she offered was very stiff.

Lucinda's eyes widened and she looked down at her feet. 'Sure. See you later.'

Opi looked away from the girl, from the offended expression, and took the stairs to the basement.

Facing Lucinda after that had been difficult. She reminded her of Rae and that hurt. Wounding the girl had been hard. It was best to stop the relationship now. Stop it from developing further. She couldn't afford to get emotionally involved. It wasn't her business. She had no right.

Lucinda was genetically her daughter. *Just like Rae. Just like Essa. I know*, she told herself. *I can't deal with it now.*

Chapter Eleven

Betrayal Most Deep

In the command centre, Opi saw that it was indeed the deadroom but with a wide metal door open to reveal the much larger room beyond. Banks of monitors were alive and kicking, with feeds showing the planet, its two moons and other places around the system.

McDevitt had his back to her and Double E was operating the control panel. Opi's gaze swept the room and she noted her handheld sat on the table where she'd left it. That was going to be necessary, so she tucked it into her body pouch, underneath her t-shirt.

At her movement, McDevitt swung around and gave her a nod of acknowledgment. Lines of worry creased his forehead and he turned back to the monitors.

Feeling fragile, Opi struggled to keep her gaze cool. McDevitt had hurt her with his distrust, although she understood it. He thought she had brought his planet into danger. She had, but not knowingly though. She was still dealing with the mortal wound to her heart. Polly had betrayed her. Every time she thought of that her stomach churned and her knees went weak. With a sigh, she told herself off. No point in reminding herself of it. It wasn't likely she'd forget.

She studied the images on the screens more closely. The viewscreens were showing scenes from various angles. Something, a ship maybe, was beaming pictures of the planet from orbit with a few others vantage points of the broader system and the jumpgate. The jumpgate shot made her nervous. It was where the space pirates would exit from. 'How many ships do you have out there?' she asked in her best executive voice.

McDevitt huffed once and turned to face her. 'None. These images are from the monitoring buoys.'

Her eyes flicked up to meet his. 'Buoys?' Why did that answer give her a sinking feeling. She remembered how they landed, how small and sparse the facilities were on Islay 2. 'How many ships do you have on this planet?'

'Just the one...'

She jerked. 'One?'

'And a backup for emergencies, although that's being overhauled right now so out of action.' He must have seen her appalled look because he continued. 'We are on a regular shipping route for transport, trade and delivery of essential items we can't supply ourselves. We don't need a fleet here.'

'No fleet. But if I don't fight the pirates in space they will come here.'

'I know. Don't worry. I have a plan.'

She stepped up close and thumped him on the shoulder. 'Don't worry? You have a plan? That's bullshit. You will risk everyone here. I have to get help.' Although she said it, she knew it wouldn't come in time. Not manned fighting ships. That hadn't been in her plans. Being on Islay 2 with McDevitt and his people had not been in her plans either. Luckily, she could adjust.

'I've got it covered, Gayens.'

Barely keeping control of her anger, she studied the screens. So she was no longer Opi. That was probably for the best anyhow. His plans wouldn't do any good. She couldn't let them sacrifice themselves.

She clenched her hands. 'No. You don't. You aren't set up for this. I have to get off this planet right away. Don't you understand?'

'Why don't you explain it to me?' His eyes were hard like lasers as they bored into hers.

'I've been tracked, bugged, betrayed. The space pirates are coming after me. They've taken the bait and that will lead them here to you.'

'Was this your plan?' he asked in a hard, flat voice. 'To bring them here?'

'My plan?' She recoiled.

'You said you had plans. Was this one of them?'

Her eyelids narrowed. 'Do you mean involve you? Your precious planet? No! No way.' She slashed the air with her hand. 'How could it be? I didn't know you were going to kidnap me and bring me here.'

Her mind was going through the options. There wasn't enough time, at least, she didn't think there was for her to call for a ship to pick her up. That bug in her goddam shoe had been broadcasting for days. Not a lot of time, but still if they were on the move it wouldn't take them long to get here. Even if she left, would that save McDevitt? Lucinda? Would that save his beautiful home? She didn't think so.

She could not allow the fight to take place on the surface of Islay 2. People would die. The place would be destroyed. McDevitt's life would be left in tatters. As much as she was wounded by his distrust, she cared enough to not want that to happen.

He studied her critically and the let out a sigh. 'Well then…looks like we are involved though doesn't it?'

'That was not my design. If you have no ships, how will you protect your people?'

'I have shields and one very big gun. We'll be all right.'

She shook her head. 'No. They won't give up. They'll just keep on coming, until you surrender me. Then because you fought them, they'll annihilate you as an example to others.'

'I'm not surrendering you so get that out of your head. Opi…' He reached out to touch her, but she backed up.

'I'm not your wife. I'm someone else entirely.'

He flinched and pulled his hand back as if stung. 'I know who and what you are. That's not why…'

'I can't let you risk this place, McDevitt. It's too…' She couldn't say it was beautiful. 'Too important. People have their livelihoods here.'

'Crops can be regrown. Houses can be rebuilt.'

'That's not the end game I'm working for here. The pirates have to be stopped. If you have no ships then you are no use to me.'

'You can't stop them, Opi. They are a force of nature. There will always be corruption.'

'Not in my company.'

His mouth lifted, not quite a smile, not quite a sneer. 'It didn't start in your company. Your company ate something that it couldn't digest.'

'You know something?'

His chin jerked up. 'More than you give me credit for.'

'I don't have time for this. Lend me your ship.'

'No. You will take shelter in the bunker when the time comes. So far there is no sign of them. We have an alert system.'

'Owain?' Double E lifted his head. 'I've got a blip. Halfway between us and the jumpgate. It's heading toward us. Whatever it is, it is heavily shielded. One burst of thrust after leaving the gate and it's just cruising.'

'Put the image up on screen. Magnify.' McDevitt sat in chair, started scanning the data coming through on one of the monitors.

The shape was long and round, made of dark grey almost black material. Opi walked behind McDevitt's chair to get a better view of it.

'What is that? I've not seen anything like it,' McDevitt asked.

'Pirate tech?' Double E suggested.

'No. It's not pirate tech,' Opi answered.

McDevitt turned toward her. 'Yours?'

'That is plan B. Fully automated minnow, shielded and ready to fire.'

'Plan B? Impressive.' His eyebrows were up and there was a glint in his eyes that showed appreciation. 'Is there a plan C?' There was no time to fraternise now.

'Keep me posted and you'll find out.'

McDevitt swung out of his seat and stepped toward her, but it was an intimacy she wasn't going to allow. She backed away. 'While the coast is clear I'm going to take a walk, get some fresh air...while there is some and maybe do some thinking.'

'It couldn't hurt,' McDevitt quipped. 'Just relax. I've got this.'

Shaking her head, Opi headed for the stairs. She could feel McDevitt's eyes on her but didn't glance back, didn't give him the satisfaction. He'd made love to her and then gutted her. It was over. Best forgotten. Why then did his eyes speak to her? Why couldn't she bear his touch? Because she wouldn't be able to think straight, that's why.

Once upstairs, she oriented herself in the house and ran down a mental to do list. First, she went into the kitchen, grabbing a water container and shoved some meal packs from the freezer into a bag. She debated leaving a note, but thought the better of it. Once she took that ship it would be obvious where she had gone and what she had done. Through the doors to the deck, she cast a wistful look at the mountains. They were beautiful and serene. She wanted to keep them that way.

Then she left the building reversing her tracks from when she walked from the ship. If a tear tracked down her cheek, she put it down to a reaction to sunlight. Too much glare was making her eyes water. It wasn't because she was leaving behind McDevitt who had touched her where no man had done since the earliest days of her infatuation with Gayens. Lucinda's face loomed large in her mind and she swiped it to the side.

The garden path meandered and she could see the fields beyond, although they were blurred by her watery eyes. Wiping her nose with the back of her hand, she powered on through the wall of grain. There was so little time to lose. The space pirates could arrive any minute and she'd been stuck there on the surface. They'd shoot her down before she left orbit. No she needed to be in position ASAP. She had to prevent them attacking the planet. She had to draw their fire.

The people on Islay 2 deserved to live. McDevitt was crazy if he thought the pirates would attack and leave without extracting her. She had to take the fight to them. Maybe then she could enact plan D and E if plan C turned up soon. Maybe she'd even think up a plan F. There was some material to work with.

Her planned showdown was not meant to include innocents. She'd had it all worked out. Her team would have been safe. The space pirates would have swarmed around her and she'd have taken them out. Now it was all at risk. Her plans shot to hell.

Nervous that McDevitt would search for her, she broke into a run. Not a health fanatic, she had some level of basic fitness. Soon she was winded and slowed back down to a jog. Perhaps he wouldn't guess her intention but she had to make sure he didn't figure it out. She paused, sipped some water and checked her surroundings. She prayed to the powers that be. Don't let them come yet. Let me get into orbit first.

When they had landed, Double E had stayed behind on the ship. She surmised that that was to make sure the ship was prepped for the next flight, log any maintenance issues, even effect repairs. That was the only thing that made sense to her. The backup ship was being repaired. McDevitt couldn't possibly depend on only two ships. But maybe he did, if his comms were that good.

Whether the ship was secured or not was her next worry. Her handheld was sitting snug in her body pouch. It didn't really matter now what she transmitted. They knew she was here. In fact, she wanted them to know that she was not here. That meant getting the ship into orbit and away from Islay 2.

She doubted McDevitt secured the ship, but she had time as she strode along, to formulate a plan if he did. One of the apps generated by her team should be able to deal with security. It was on her handheld. Provided she'd managed to keep hold of her handheld or was able to access some sort of system with wider network she'd be fine. Her VesperNet held it all. Any access would give her the ability to use her apps provided she could prove her identity. But as her handheld was in her custody, she should have no trouble.

Very soon the ship was in view. Leaning over with her hands on her knees, she caught her breath. That had been some distance she'd covered in a pretty short time. She visually scanned the ship, checking for signs that it was unserviceable. As she walked closer, she saw that it was intact and there were no signs of repairs in progress.

At the sight of the extended landing ramp, her heart gave a little leap. The ship was open. Yet at the top of the ramp she saw the door was shut. She climbed up the ramp and palmed the lock. It blinked red and the door didn't budge.

Who would have thought it? McDevitt had locked the ship.

Extracting her handheld, she keyed up the app. She tried an initial pass, hoping her software would handshake with the ship's so she could unkey the lock. On the second try, she thumped the ship's panel. The bloody thing was shielded.

'I said you couldn't borrow my ship.' McDevitt's voice sounded behind her.

She jumped and guiltily swung around. 'What are you doing here? Following me?' Then she thought the space pirates must have passed through the jumpgate. 'Have they...?'

He lifted his hand. 'No. They aren't through yet.'

Her shoulders sagged. 'McDevitt.' Then sucking in a breath she lifted her gaze to his. 'Owain. I need to get into orbit. My plans depend upon it.'

'So you remember my name after all. I thought you'd mislaid it.'

Her eyes narrowed. 'What do you want? I can buy your ship. Replace it with a new one.'

He shook his head. 'You don't get it do you. Your money means nothing to me. You can't go up in my ship. You can't pilot it.'

Frustration was building inside her. 'I can pilot it.'

He scoffed. 'On automatic. Automatic will kill you up there. Face it, you can't go up alone.'

She cast her gaze around seeking inspiration. 'Alone?' She shook her head. 'No. You can't come with me. You have a daughter who loves you, needs you. It's likely a one way trip.'

'And you expect me to stand by and let you take that trip alone? Let you die defending me and mine? No way.'

Opi decided to hit below the belt. 'Oh is your male ego dented that a mere woman might be capable?'

He surged forward and nudged her out of the way, nearly knocking her off the ramp. He keyed the lock and spoke harshly. 'You are too stupid for words at times.'

He entered the ship and disappeared inside. She ran after him. 'Look, you can't come with me. I won't let you.'

He turned to her, nose to nose. 'You can't stop me.'

Opi wished she'd had the foresight to bring a weapon. She could have stunned him, dragged him outside and left him to be toasted by the engine blast while he ate her dust. Alas, she had no weapon.

She stomped down the companion way after him. He took the command seat and started the pre-flight systems' check. Opi still too angry for words, grabbed the check list and assisted him.

'Hatch seal in one minute,' she said. 'Last chance to bail.'

He shot her a dirty look. 'Keep that up and I'll toss you out the hatch once we take off. It's a long way down.'

Opi laughed. 'Yeah right.'

McDevitt laughed too. 'You think I'm kidding.'

'Yes.'

'Then let's just say that I'll put you over my knee and paddle your backside if I get any more lip from you.'

'Understood, sir.'

'Ready to engage. Strap in.'

'Strapped in.' The console lights keyed on. Red, yellow and then green. 'Fuel is green.' She checked the labels. Life support was green, engine green. 'Weapons...weapons? I didn't realise your ship was armed.' She cast him a sideways look.

He turned his head, grinned evilly and punched in the launch sequence. 'There's a lot you don't know about me, Gayens. A lot.' He engaged the ignition and the ship shuddered and then he leant on the throttle and the ship moved.

Then there was no time for talking as the ship began lift off. Gravity forced her back into her seat and the ship bucked and rocked as it fought the atmosphere. The ship was tilting to a forty five degree angle and then it shot up, suddenly free of the constraints of atmosphere and gravity. Opi shut her eyes and tried to keep her mouth from falling open and back as they picked up speed.

Once they had reached orbit, McDevitt asked, 'Where to?'

'Set course toward the jumpgate.' She pulled out her link. Her heart thudded. McDevitt set the course. 'Now I'm hoping your ship has an escape pod.'

He kept his eyes on the controls and engaged the thrusters for a burst of speed. 'I do.'

'Then you need to use it. Right now.'

He cast her a sideways look. 'This is my ship. I'm the captain and the captain goes down with his ship.'

Opi thumped her hand on the console. 'No, damn you! You do not go down with the ship. That is not part of the plan.'

'Fuck your plans.'

Recoiling, she just glared at him. Words fought with each other to get out of her mouth and all she could do was bite down on them. They were coming up on Islay's smaller moon. Her mind worked furiously. If he jettisoned himself here he'd have a chance. She extracted her handheld. Called up her shipping agent order sheet and executed orders for two ships to be delivered to Islay 2, pronto. They weren't going to get there in time to be useful but they'd replace this one eventually and give him more options on backups. Then she had a thought. 'What are your account details? I'll buy this ship from you.'

McDevitt shook his head, a pitying expression on his face. 'Your money is not going to help you here. This ship is not for sale.'

Opi keyed off her handheld and stared out the viewport. Controlling her anger wasn't easy. 'Goddamit. You don't know what you are getting into.'

A crooked smile crossed his features. 'I think I do. Course set for jumpgate.'

Opi tried again. She wasn't used to other people fighting her battles. It grated. It was uncomfortable and he could die. 'But this is such a waste. You have a family, a life...'

'And a job.'

Opi fell back against her seat, gutted. 'A job?' she asked. It was as if the deck had fallen away beneath her. All kinds of scenarios went through her brain. He was working for them. He was out to get her... Erase that. Ask him the question woman.

'What job?'

Chapter Twelve

Space Battle

Instead of answering, he keyed the comms. 'Double E?'

'Standing by.'

'Everyone under cover?'

'Yes sir. All present and accounted for. Weapons are primed.'

'Good wait for my signal.'

Opi thumped the console again. 'I'm the job, aren't I?'

'Hey, don't damage the ship.' He rubbed the spot where her hand had impacted. 'You aren't the job. We're on the same job, except you cut me out...unknowingly, I expect, out of the running.'

Opi grabbed handfuls of her hair and pulled. 'What are you talking about?' Her mind turned over the information at hand quickly. She'd bought him out. His company was a big, fat duck waiting to be plucked. Then she locked gazes with him. 'Your holdings were a set up to lure pirates. You never retired.'

His grin grew wider. 'Close. Real close.'

She studied him. 'Who funded you to go under cover?'

His eyebrow lifted. 'I'm government, Ms Gayens. In case you hadn't heard before I'll advise you now, the government doesn't like private individuals interfering in law enforcement matters.'

Opi studied his serious face for a minute. Then she burst out laughing.

McDevitt opened his mouth, a gape of surprised confusion. 'Why are you laughing?' He checked his controls. 'This is a serious operation.'

It took a few moments to get herself under control. 'Because the government is helping me. Obviously, a different arm of government or maybe not.' She threw up her hands. 'Who knows.'

'You know,' he said. 'You're actually smarter than I thought, and I thought you were pretty smart.' His gaze travelled down her body. 'You're also way calmer than you ought to be. What gives?'

His voice was soft, seductive and despite outward appearances, she responded to it. A surge of warmth swept over her. Suddenly emotion was close to the surface. He had no idea what was ahead. 'Owain, you can't be here. I hadn't factored you into this scenario.'

He reached over and squeezed her hand. 'Opi. I'm staying. Reconfigure your plans.' His voice was soft, hushed as if he didn't want the universe to hear. 'You need me.'

Meeting his direct gaze she said, 'I can't. It's too late now. It's set in motion.'

There was something soft there in his eyes, concern, affection, love. Her eyes widened. No, it couldn't be that. It was his clone he was seeing. Not her.

'It all leads to here.'

The expression in his eyes grew hard. 'Last stand?' His fists clenched and all traces of softness left his voice 'Is that the best you can do?' he demanded harshly. 'Make yourself goddamn bait?'

'Yes, it's the best I can do! I can't let anyone else to put their lives on the line.'

He thumped the console this time. 'Do better. Damn it.'

'What business is it of yours?'

His eyebrows flew up. 'You ask me that now? Bloody hell, Opi. This may be your plan but I'm making it my business. It's my job to apprehend the pirates and make sure they get prosecuted. There has to be another way.'

She shook her head. 'No, Owain, you don't understand. I **am** the bait. I'm the blade that lances the boil. I'm too tempting a target to miss.'

Owain grabbed her, pulled her out of her chair. 'I won't let you do this.'

'You can't stop me.'

'I can.' His teeth clenched and a growl of frustration escaped his mouth.

'You won't. You know this is our best chance. You'll see they'll send everything they have at me.'

'No, Opi...listen to reason.'

The ship's comms engaged. It was Double E. 'We have confirmed sighting of multiple ships exiting the jumpgate. Current count twenty and rising.'

Opi turned on her comm link. She needed the pirates to know she was on this ship.

Her comms link beeped. 'Incoming call,' she said. 'On screen.'

Her personal unit directed to the main monitor.

She hesitated, breathed to calm down. Just as she engaged the unit to answer, McDevitt reached for her, crushed his mouth against hers. It was so unexpected that Opi went along with it, enjoyed this one last moment of lust that surged up inside. 'Ms Gayens?' It was Polly.

McDevitt lifted away from her and she smiled at him stupidly, before turning to face her traitorous assistant. 'Polly. Finally. My stupid link has been playing up. What's the status?'

Polly grinned at her. 'Hot date I see. Mueller thought you'd been kidnapped.'

'No, I went along voluntarily.'

Opi tried to see beyond the eyes, beyond the facade of the slightly ditzy assistant.

Polly's hair was now electric blue and drawn up into stiff points. Her eyes glittered mischievously. 'Did you get laid?'

'I got laid very well indeed.'

'That's great. I have a surprise for you. Hold on a minute.' Polly reached down and brought up Mueller's severed head. The Polly she knew had disappeared. There was a manic gleam in this woman's eye and a savage smile on her face.

'Oh god!' Opi's hands covered her mouth.

Polly leant forward so her face dominated the viewer. 'He was a traitor. Did you know? He betrayed us.'

The cards were on the table. Opi tried not to look at Mueller's expression. He'd suffered before dying. Damn Polly.

'Us? Not me personally?'

Polly dropped the head and it floated slowly down. 'Yes, you. Of course it was you he betrayed.'

They locked gazes, a sizzle of static interfering with the feed now and then. 'You bought me the shoes, Polly.'

'Mueller made me bug them. I was acting under his orders.'

Opi shook her head. So Polly knew about the bug. 'No, Polly, Mueller would have told me what he'd done. We had an agreed procedure.'

The layers of pretence fell away. Before her eyes, Polly changed into something more, something dark and mean. 'Well, fuck him,' Polly yelled at the screen. Then she kicked, presumably at Mueller's severed head. 'I've come to collect you, Ms Gayens. You're late for an important appointment.'

Opi lifted her chin. 'Am I? I thought I was right on time.'

Polly's face changed again, almost the old Polly, the friend Polly, and then she sneered and it was the evil Polly again. 'You won't win this one. They know you too well. Your strengths, your weaknesses. They know how to surprise you.'

Opi let her eyes stray to the vidfeed from Double E. 'You brought an awful lot of ships to collect me, Polly. Bit of an overkill.'

The feed from McDevitt's buoys showed a motley array of ships. She was aghast at how many were emblazoned with the AllEarth Corp logo. They were pouring out of the jumpgate. Opi grinned. They were arrayed along the elliptical plane. No imagination. No three D awareness. Unless that changed as it well might. She had to be careful to keep them there.

Polly's expression altered. 'I'm glad you got laid before you die. I didn't think you had it in you.'

'I'm sorry it has come to this, Pol. We were friends.'

Polly laughed, a derisive tone that cut into Opi's already broken heart. 'Yeah, right. Well, get this bitch,' she poked a finger at the screen. 'I'm sorry I can only kill your sorry ass once.'

Opi lurched and near fell out of her seat as the ship dived underneath her feet. 'What are you doing?' she hissed at McDevitt.

'Evasive manoeuvres!' Came the shouted reply.

'I didn't give you any orders to evade.' Opi struggled back into her seat and fumbled with the straps of her seat belt.

'It's my ship. I'm in command.'

'Trouble in paradise?' Polly sneered. 'Good bye.' She turned to the side. 'Engage.' Then the comms cut.

'You will ruin everything?' A blast careened of their starboard bow. Her eyes widened and her heart jumped. If they'd stayed in place it would have been a direct hit.

McDevitt was busily piloting the ship on an erratic course. 'How? By keeping us alive?'

'They aren't all through yet. I want them all here and closer to us.'

'Closer? You're nuts. That assistant of yours nearly fried us. I can pretty much guarantee that the rest of those ships are prepped to do the same thing.'

'I know, but look at their formation. All arrayed on the same plane. I need to keep them there as long as possible.'

McDevitt confirmed her assessment with a tight nod and a firm mouth. 'Can you contact Double E?'

McDevitt hit a switch. 'E?'

'Receiving.'

Opi took over the conversation. 'Hi, Double E. Has anything else come through the gate? A package marked especially for me?'

There was silence on the line. 'Yes.'

'Can you confirm position?'

'I'll send the coordinates through.'

'Thanks. Out.'

'There is over a hundred ships here.' McDevitt checked his scans. 'There jamming their IDs. Are all of them pirates?'

Opi pulled on her bottom lip. 'I think so. They better be. Plan B and C are pretty indiscriminate. They can fire in a three sixty rotation but I'm thinking concentrated thirty-three degree angle fire front and back.'

She took up her handheld. Entered in the keycodes to activate her minnows. 'McDevitt?'

'Yes,' he ground out, his eyes on the tactical displays and the ship's controls.

'How soon can you drop up us ninety degrees up or down and give us a five kilometre distance from the main formation of the ships?'

He cast her a look, frowned when he saw the handheld. 'You going for Plan B?'

Opi grinned. 'And plan C?'

'Show me.'

Opi brought up the virtual scenario and he nodded grimly. 'How much time can you give me?' he asked.

'Once I engage it will take three minutes for full deployment.'

'And where do we need to be after that?'

Opi was glad he had seen plan B and C for what they were. Thinners. Now she needed to get the remainder of the pirate fleet concentrated on her and not Islay 2. 'We need to come up in the centre. The remaining ships will surround us and concentrate their fire. Can you get us there?'

He nodded and shook his head. 'Damn me. I thought you were just a pretty face.'

The ship dove into a spiral heading away from the elliptic. It looked like an attack run. They'd be tracking them, making projections on where they'd come about. Let them. As long as they didn't' follow the *Matilda* and break formation. 'Not bad. And I thought you were just good in bed.'

He chuckled as he shot their ship at full speed into the centre of a ship storm but doing it out of range of her automated and covert firing system, her minnows.

Polly came shouting through comms. 'Are you crazy? You aren't getting away, Gayens. I've got you surrounded. Fire!'

The closest ships altered their positions. They were no longer heading for the planet but were aligning themselves with McDevitt's ship. Others she could see were forming up in front of the jumpgate to block their escape. Plan C was right behind them.

'Easy. We need to keep them pretty well on this plane. If they break up, dive or climb, then we are in for a shit fight.'

'I'm ready.' The ship bucked as it was hit by stray fire. McDevitt was using evasive manoeuvres.

'Now, now.' He yelled and blurted fire out of his onboard weapons. Spurts of blue flame spat out and caught a couple of ships dropping down out of formation to follow them.

A virtual console filled the screen of her handheld. She hit the command button. One light flashed green as it received her message. The other showed red. 'Come on,' she growled. Then the other light changed to green.

'Brace yourself.' She cried out.

The blast shields closed over their viewport. Opi lifted an eyebrow. That wasn't going to help much. 'On screen.'

The ships were trying to adjust to their new position. A few had broken off to follow their trajectory. The ship bucked as they took fire.

Opi saw the damage report flash up on screen. 'Damn and blast. I take it you can't pilot and fire arms. Do you want me to take over?'

McDevitt's hands flew over the console. 'No. I'm on it. Tell me when.'

They were gaining—three ships hot on their tail. 'Fire at will.'

'Engaging, cluster fire,' he yelled.

One of the ships disappeared from screen. Another slowed. The other closed on their position fast. 'Evasive manoeuvres.' McDevitt said and sent the ship into another downward spiral.

'It's coming.'

'What are those things? Some kind of secret weapon?' His attention appeared to focus everywhere at once, on the ships controls, weapons, her.

'Yes.'

There was a flash on the viewscreen then it went dark. Then their systems died. 'Gayens?' McDevitt frantically tried to reinitialise his onboard systems. 'What have you done?'

She put a hand on his forearm. 'Just give it a minute. We've only got the spill over. We were not in the direct line of fire.'

'Damn...are they dead? Destroyed?'

Opi glanced at him eyes wide. 'Are you asking me if I murdered thousands of people in cold blood?'

His eyebrows furrowed and he swallowed before replying. 'Yes.'

She shook her head. 'No doubt there will be some casualties. It can't be predicted where people are, what they are doing when the minnow's beam hits.'

McDevitt key the manual release on the blast doors. 'Let's see what we've got here.'

'That blast fried all their circuits. Melted them to sludge. It overloads all onboard power.'

'You think you got all of them?'

She shook her head. 'No, but I'm hoping most of them were in range.'

Their view was from bottom up. A large ship was in the process of colliding with its neighbour. Debris spilled out from where the metal of the two ships tried to occupy the same space. The larger ship sliced through the smaller ones. Opi thought she saw bodies in the wreckage.

McDevitt winced and pulled back his head as he studied the scene. 'That's got to hurt.'

Opi leant forward, trying to keep up a visual scan out the viewport and on the scopes. 'Keep a look out,' she said. 'We still have a ship on our tail. Once we regain power so will they. Then there are those that didn't get caught in the minnows' fire.'

Console lights began to glow steady as each system commenced restart. Opi checked the readouts on the status display. She configured the sensors to scan for live ships. Her heart thumped as she watched the display. Then they came, blip after blip. More than she'd wished for. The sensor sweep continued. More indicators blinked. There was a section on the periphery that missed the full force of the blast. 'About fifteen ships survived full internal meltdown. Are comms still down?'

McDevitt flicked a switch. 'Yes.'

'Mmm and the ship that was attacking us?'

'Can't see it on the scope. It could be right under us or behind us. Shit!' he exclaimed. McDevitt undid his seat belt and climbed out of his seat.

'What are you doing?' she asked.

He pressed his face to the viewport. 'Visual scanning. We have momentum and we don't want to be careening into another ship like those two out there.' He climbed down and went to another viewport. Nose flattened to the plate.

'Power is coming up,' she said reading the indicator and the increasing brightness of the console's display.

McDevitt climbed back into his seat. 'Then stand by to engage. I have plotted a course. Provided we are free and clear, we move.'

Opi leant over and checked his course coordinates. It was just a random course from what she could see. He wasn't trying to take them back to Islay 2. He wasn't trying to stymie her plans. Letting out a breath, she didn't realise she was holding, she knew she could trust him. For the moment, at least. Gradually systems came back on line. They weren't up to engine start as yet.

For a moment she reflected that she was in a better position than she had bargained for. McDevitt had given her an edge. He was a better pilot than she was and kept a cool head. If she'd been piloting on her own plan B with plan C would have left her floating out there disabled and waiting for the government forces to pick them all up. Minus those ships that escaped or hung around to destroy her first, which is what they had come for after all.

It may not have been a full lancing of the boil she had hoped for, but she would have taken the top off it. And she had Polly. Her mole. Her two-faced executive assistant. If she hadn't seen Polly with Mueller's head, she wouldn't have believed it in a million years. Even with the shoes as evidence against her.

Polly could have talked her around with the shoe bug, could have come up with a number of excuses, lies that Opi would have bought because she wanted to. It was easier than believing the worst. Shaking her head, she realised she didn't want the traitor to be Polly. It hurt too damn much.

Her handheld was dead. She engaged the restart button but it was beyond fixing. Damn. Her comm link was better shielded. She needed to extract Polly's tendrils from AllEarth Corp right now. Rescind all permissions. Freeze all accounts. Cut her off!

She unbuckled from her seat and went to the comms unit. 'This is Opeia Gayens,' she said into the pickup. Her screen showed nothing but black snow. She double checked the comms system which she was trying to relay through. No voice. No visuals. Emergency text only. She got busy keying. One code stream would lock everybody but her out of critical systems.

McDevitt shouted. 'Opi!'

'What?' Opi turned and saw what was in the viewscreen.

The thruster was blinking green. 'Engage! Engage!' McDevitt shouted as he keyed in changes to their course.

Opi slammed her hand down on the control. The shipped bucked, twirled and spun up and then out to the side. Her handheld flew out of her hands and she barely held onto the chair. 'Jesus.'

McDevitt's swearing reached her. He was flat against the ceiling. Thank god he was all right.

He came back in pulling himself along by his hands, feet flailing behind. Once back in the command chair, he glared at her and she shifted back to her own seat. 'That was close,' he said taking his seat once again. Facing her, he put his hands about a foot apart. 'We were that close.'

'Collision?'

He nodded and the controls drew his concentration once again. He'd set up a series of manoeuvres and saved them.

Opi raised her eyebrows in surprise and hoped that he was in fact exaggerating.

'How did you do that? Get us out in time. Engine is not up yet.'

'I keyed a series of thruster moves. They are on a different line and power has restored. See?'

Opi nodded. 'I wouldn't have thought of that. I would have been a sitting duck. I didn't even factor in the drift. I was never any good at physics.'

'You don't have military experience. You're smart but you can't think of everything.'

'I know.' She stared out the viewscreen, winced as another pair of ships in the distance tried to occupy the same space.

'Well?'

'Well what?' she asked, chewing her bottom lip.

'Aren't you going to admit that you needed me?'

She turned to him, a slight smile playing about her lips. For her it was such a loaded question. She didn't want to encourage him. She wanted him far from harm. But there was nothing she could do about it. 'I'd be dead without you, Owain.'

He sighed and his eyes glittered as they studied her. 'We aren't done yet.'

'If only the government ships would hurry up. They must have known where the battle would take place because of the deployment of the minnows.'

McDevitt scanned the array of ships. 'How long before pickup?'

'The minnows signal back to government headquarters when they engage. Not too long. A day. Maybe two. Depending on how much of a hurry they are and where they staged operations.'

McDevitt's gaze stared out the port. 'A few people could die before then.'

She nodded. 'We could be among them.' Her voice was steady. 'We have live ships. Like us they are reinitialising systems and then the battle will begin, again.'

He grinned like a lunatic. 'You've got balls, Gayens.'

Opi chuckled. 'So do you McDevitt.' She dropped her gaze and raised an eyebrow.

He shook his head. 'Timing, Opi.'

'Yeah. Anymore juice in those weapons of yours?'

'On board, no.'

The monitor showed ships dropping out of the elliptic plane and making a beeline for their position. These ships appeared to have been sheltered from the blast by other ships in the formation. 'We have hot ones on our tail,' he said. 'Ideas?'

'Stay alive?'

'Right. So maybe I can use a plan or two of my own? Now that your self-sacrifice is done.'

She turned and met his eye. 'I didn't say I was done yet. I'm working on it. If you can keep us alive for a while, I'll get on it. By the way, comms is down to emergency text only. I'm hoping that lot have no comms as well.'

He studied the screen, watching the ships form up. 'I'd say they have ship to ship.'

'And us?'

'I have what I need. Strap yourself in. We're going for a ride.'

'Sounds good.'

'You know…did you really enjoy it?'

Opi's cheeks heated up. 'What?' she asked although she knew exactly what he meant.

'You know…you told that traitorous bitch that you got well laid. Did you? Or were you just hamming it up?'

Opi clenched her fists. 'Now isn't the time to discuss this.'

His head jerked back and she could see that she'd hurt him. 'When is a better time? After we're dead?'

Opi chewed her lip and shook her head. 'Have it your way. But you're taking a big risk. What if I said you were a dud lay. What then?'

His eyes widened, but his mouth was curved up cheekily. 'Was I?'

'You know damn well you weren't.' She poked him in the shoulder three times. 'If anything I was the one lagging behind.'

'Nothing of the kind. But practice makes perfect. I can help you out there.'

'You sure can.'

A slow grin spread over his face as he keyed the controls. 'Oh in that case, we better live.' He turned to her. 'I can do better. Much better.' His eyes jerked up and down and then with a theatrical show he punched in the engine start. 'Engines engaged. Hold tight.'

'McDevitt you're an idiot, but I like you.'

He sent her a feral grin. He was seriously deranged. She checked their trajectory. 'Um…McD…Owain why are we headed toward your second moon? I want to lead them away from your planet.'

'Shut up, Opi. I'm in charge now.'

Opi swore in the most unladylike fashion she could think of. His grin grew wider. 'Incoming fire.' He yelled and the ship buckled. The cockpit sealed itself automatically. Opi leant forward and checked the damage readouts. 'Hull breach. Aft sections.' She shook her head.

'I know.'

'Where're the escape pods?'

'Here. Just one left now.' He punched a control above his head. Masks fell out. 'Put one of these on.'

She took one and hooked it around her neck. 'Great. You better get in it. We take another hit like that and this ship is toast.'

McDevitt put his mask around his neck. 'No. You get ready and get in it. Shit's about to happen.'

Opi sat back, gaping at him open mouthed. 'What shit?'

'Double E?'

'Yes, sir.'

'Anything happening at the jumpgate? Reinforcements?'

'You have comms back? You didn't say.' She angled her mask so that she could flick it up over her mouth and nose when needed.

Double E's voice came through comms and Opi had to put off her rant so she could listen. 'Sorry, I'll check. I was keeping an eye on you lot. You have ten live ships headed your way. They'll make contact in five minutes. Let me see. Nothing so far.' There was a pause. 'Wait a minute. Something is coming through.' A loud whistle sounded through the speaker. 'Big government ship, possibly military.' There was a break in transmission and then Double E's voice sounded through the speaker. 'It's not broadcasting any identifiers.'

McDevitt caught her eye, lifting his eyebrows. 'Running on silent? Were you expecting support to be clandestine? I thought the government would want to broadcast their triumph.'

Opi swallowed, a bad feeling in her gut. 'Yes, I agree. Big bells ringing and all that,' she replied carefully as if speaking would break reality. She lifted her link to signal. 'I'll contact them and see.'

McDevitt placed his hand over hers, preventing her and shook his head. 'Like you,' he said. 'I was expecting blaring trumpets and a fleet of press ships dancing to the fanfare. This is seriously sus.'

Opi agreed, but couldn't rearrange her thinking enough to believe. 'Give it a few seconds. Let's see what unfolds.'

There was a bright white flash outside the viewport. 'What just happened?' she asked.

McDevitt checked the scope. 'Don't know. Double E can you give me a status report?'

There was another flash, white tinged, then blue. A ship's atmosphere exploding? Opi gulped. She had a bad feeling deep in her belly. 'Sir, they appear to be vaporising the incapacitated craft, starting with those nearest the jumpgate.'

'What? No!' Opi exploded in rage and shock. 'That's not what's supposed to happen. They are meant to bring them on board to apprehend them, not kill them.'

McDevitt frowned as another flash flared briefly. 'Tell me was part of the plan to interrogate the prisoners? You know, to find out who the other pirates are, what the connections in…say…government might be?'

Tears leaked from her eyes as she stared at Owain. For a moment she couldn't speak. Could betrayal spread that far to her contacts? She swallowed and then sniffed. 'Isn't that standard procedure? The space pirates are the biggest conspiracy after all.'

McDevitt nodded and rubbed his chin as he looked out the viewport, another flash making his face appear flat as the hollows of his bone structure were overridden 'I think we should stay quiet.' Flicking a few switches, he powered down the engines and turned off all unnecessary systems. Even life support was now on standby.

'What no!' She put her hand on his, pleading eyes locking with his. 'I can't let them do that. I just can't. Please, we have to do something. They are sitting ducks out there.' Another flash, larger and more brilliant than the rest. The light reflected off McDevitt's blue eyes as he stared at the ships outside, chewing his bottom lip.

A bigger ship, lots of crew, more people on her conscience. Again she lifted the link. 'There could be innocent people on board and to hell with the links to the whole set up.'

'Think.' He held up a hand. 'If you let them know where we are then they will wipe us too. Along with all the rest. We will achieve nothing but an early death.'

'But…' She wiped at the tears of frustration spilling down her cheeks. 'Oh no!'

'What? You suspect who's responsible, right?'

She nodded and sniffed loudly. 'They are clearing out the whole thing. Damn it! It has to be Burr. Senator Burr. He supplied the minnows. He knew my plans, although he doubted it would work.'

McDevitt grinned as he faced her and his eyes sparkled. 'You have your man.' He slapped her on the knee.

She pushed his hand away. 'Not without evidence I don't.' She pointed out the viewport. 'My evidence is being extinguished while I do nothing to stop it. Stop him.' She wrung her hands and swore. 'He's been in it the whole time. Years! Damn it he comforted me when my parents died.' The past reordered itself quickly with this new information. He'd been helping Carl with the clones. It all made sense now. He'd covered his tracks until now. Then she saw the writing on the wall. He'd have to control her or end her.

'I have a plan.' She locked gazes with McDevitt.

McDevitt pulled a face, scrunching up his lips in a pout. 'What plan?'

'Give me a minute and then I will cue you.'

'I'm risking a lot backing you in this. But I'm there. Go for it.'

The incursion of the large warship had distracted their attackers. McDevitt manning the scanners gave her an update. Six ships had broken off to engage the government destroyer. They were vaporised in quick order. That left one ship hot on their tail with three more coming in. The closest one got off a shot just to remind them that they were still there.

'I bet you, Polly is on that ship.'

McDevitt didn't look up from what he was doing. 'I agree. Now, use your link and hail that ship. Give them a raspberry and tell them to come get you. I'll keep Miss Polly off our tail.'

He re-engaged the engines, moving them on thrusters to keep from being blasted apart. The ship shuddered and there was a creak. 'Was that part of the ship coming loose?'

'Yes. You'd better suit up.'

'What about you?' He unstrapped himself and started donning his emergency spacesuit which was stored in the cupboard next to his seat. He tossed away the emergency mask. It wasn't going to cope with vacuum, which is what she suspected they were facing. Opi found a suit in the cupboard below the command console right near her own seat.

He gave her a nod and she keyed the link. 'This is Opeia Gayens of AllEarth Corp. Please desist from destroying these disabled craft. I have an authorised operation in progress. I repeat desist.'

Another flare greeted her response. 'Damn them to hell and back.'

McDevitt's voice fed directly into her ear piece. 'My thoughts exactly. Miss Polly has ceased firing. I'd say she is weighing up her options. The government ship is still flying silent and is blocking access to the jumpgate.'

'Double E. Any change in position?'

'Yes, sir. They are moving slowly. Calculating their trajectory now. They are accelerating. Slowly at first but building momentum. Ah...they are heading straight for you.'

'Good. We are the bait. You get me E?'

'Yes sir. I'm tracking you.'

'Stand ready.'

'Yes, sir.'

McDevitt did a loop, leaving Polly's ship out in the open and then backtracked toward the second moon. Opi had no idea what he was up to.

'How long to intercept?'

He didn't look up from the controls. 'Not long now. We just have to keep Miss Polly entertained.' He hit fire control and three laser bolts shot from their ship. One hit the other ship dead on. 'Eat that.' McDevitt winked at Opi. At least she thought he did. Through their helmet it was hard to read facial expressions.

Opi read the display. 'Not destroyed. Systems overload. It may take her a few minutes to deal with that.'

'Double E, are we ready to party?'

'Yes, sir. Tracking.'

'Do we have company?'

'Yes, sir. It a lumbering behemoth. Oh damn. It just took out another of the live ships.' Double E hummed a bit then came back on speaker. 'I've done some calculations, Owain. I don't think this hot dog is going to fit into the bun. It's thick skinned, heavily armoured. Any chance of going round for a second pass to squeeze some sauce?'

'What are you talking about?' Opi demanded into her comm link. Double E didn't answer fast enough. 'McDevitt?'

'Stand by E.'

'He's saying the ship is big and well armoured. We may not be able to disable it in one shot. Wants to know if we can survive long enough for a second run. I'm thinking not.'

'Right.' She shook her head and meaningly gestured to their wrecked ship.

With a nod to her, he reengaged the comms. 'Don't think so. We are going to have to have a dry hot dog. We are only going to get one chance at this and the *Matilda* isn't going to make another pass. She's cactus as it is.'

'Sir, they are charging weapons. They have long range plasma cannons.'

'Hold on!'

McDevitt twisted the ship, spiralled it up and around and the came up behind Polly's temporarily disabled ship, using it for cover.

'Status?'

'They are still closing. But holding fire.'

'Yeah, looks like Polly is not expendable. For now at least. We in range yet?' They had left Polly's ship behind but it still blocked the direct line of fire. The government ship would have to get closer.

'No sir, you are nearing target range.'

'Get ready to fire.'

'But sir, I can't... You'll be caught.'

'Yes, you can. I'm going to dart through on full power. Stay on bloody target.'

'Damn you!' Opi exploded, just realising what McDevitt was up to. All the time he was pretending to follow her plan and he had one of his own. She thought they were going to fire on the ship, but it was Double E using a hidden weapon. 'You have a bloody gun on that moon. Why didn't you say? I could have figured it into the plan.'

'You didn't tell me your plans. Why should I tell you mine? You know the rule. You show me yours, I'll show you mine.' His grin was evil.

Opi narrowed her gaze, not helpful in the helmet. 'That's a stupid thing to say. You knew what I was up against.'

He threw up his gloved hand. 'How? You didn't tell me!'

'You knew. I was the job.'

McDevitt growled and it sounded loud through the ear piece. 'How many times do I have to say it? You weren't the job!' he yelled at her. 'Get it. You were not the job.' He jabbed a finger at the viewscreen. 'They were. They were the job, goddammit.'

Tears threatened to spill over as she nodded. 'I get it, Owain McDevitt. I get it. I believe you.'

All the tension left his body. He leant forward, put his hands on the side her helmet to tilt it forward. He blew her a kiss, right where her forehead would be. 'Thank you for saying that. I can die happy now that we understand each other.' He released her and thumped a switch. A light flashed above the escape pod. 'Now get in the goddamn pod.'

Opi's gaze assessed it. 'It's big enough for two.'

'So what. You need to get clear.'

'I'm not going, Owain. Not without you.'

'Don't fight me on this.' He grabbed her by the upper arms manhandled her. She kicked and bucked. 'I'm in charge now. This is my plan. Look out for Lucinda for me.'

'No! You look out for her yourself. She needs you.'

She clung to the opening of the pod as he tried to push her inside. He wasn't succeeding.

'Are you always this difficult?' He eased off trying to shove her into the pod and regarded her, hands on hips, mouth a tight line.

'Of course.' Pride stiffened her spine. 'I'm Opeia Gayens head of AllEarth Corp. People listen to me.' She used the back of the seat to float away from the escape pod.

An alarm sounded. McDevitt dived onto the command console. 'Incoming fire. Brace for impact.'

The ship shuddered. McDevitt studied his read out. Flames erupted from the command console. Auto fire systems spurted mist over the controls. 'Polly has powered up again. We're losing power.' He read another screen. 'Oh shit.'

'What?'

He studied the screen a bit longer, clicked a switch and swore mightily. 'The big one is getting close. I detect a build-up of power in their weapons systems.'

'How much closer do you need them to be for your cannon to take them out?'

'Look up my skirt close. We need them tailing us into the line of fire. We get one shot at this. If we miss, they turn then guns on the moon, then Islay 2.'

He frowned at the screen. 'They going to shoot in about...now.'

Opi used the grips to help her get over to the escape pod. She hit the prep button.

'You changed your mind?' he asked.

'No. We both go. There's too much slack in the plan. No point in dying for it if we can't seal the deal.'

'It's too close. The pod will get caught too,' he observed.

'Maybe, give a spurt of speed, empty the tanks. Whatever. Just do it now. Get us out of range of your cannon. Then that government cruiser will need to readjust their course to target us. They'll speed up.'

He locked gazes with her and nodded. She ship lurched, stuttered and then moved. Two second later the weapons fire hit. Opi had McDevitt by the hand and tugged. Fire swept through the ship, the bulkhead buckled and ripped. McDevitt was thrown back and floated unmoving. She dragged on his limp form with pure desperation. When he was in the pod, she hit the eject button.

The door seal came down, locked with a thunk. Then the thrusters shot them away from the ship, which blew apart in a ball of flame that licked the edges of the pod's single viewport. McDevitt hung limply, leaning against her body. 'Owain?'

Quietening her panic, she tried to listen for his breathing, but there was nothing coming through her comm link. The pod turned end over end, drawn by the planet's gravity. Opi cried. She screamed but it made no difference. No one could hear her.

Owain didn't move. Opi feared he was dead. A bright light seared across her vision. The cannon. The escape pod accelerated, caught up in the blast wave, and then tumbled faster. Debris flew across her vision. It was amazing that they hadn't been struck or taken out in the blast. A red light flashed in her helmet. She read the display as a warning tone engaged. Her spacesuit was running out of air. She was going to die. They were going to die.

What annoyed her most was that she was going to die without knowing if she'd won the battle with the space pirates and that she didn't have time to get Senator Burr behind bars.

Chapter Thirteen

Aftermath

Pain. It filled her mind. Something touched her. Fire blossomed in her nerves and then it was gone. Light. Pain. Touch. It hurt so much. There was nothing but sharp excruciating thrusts that filled her awareness, stole her breath, filled every cell with extreme agony.

Time was all now. That moment. That intense need to breathe, to breathe through the discomfort. Then the painful sensations faded. Her head though was befuddled, gluggy and she couldn't focus. *Just breathe. Breathe.*

A headache so momentous she thought her head had been smashed in and the pieces put together with very flimsy tape. If she moved the pieces would fall out. Her hand would go there automatically to hold the piece in place. All she knew was that she was alive before she lost consciousness again.

'Opi?' A voice called out to her. She screwed up her face. That sounded like Rae. Rae was somewhere else. Darkness like liquid smothered her for some time.

'Opi?' Opi detected a lightness on the other side of her closed eyelids, a sickening, lurid pink. 'Opi?' the voice was more urgent. Was that Rae?

'Rae?' she said through a dry mouth and a throat ready to close up.

'No. It's Lucinda.'

'Lucinda?' At first Opi's mind wouldn't work. Where was she? She must open her eyes. *Danger! Danger!* Self-preservation kicked in.

Lucinda's face came into focus. Opi's eyes darted around the room. It was familiar. 'Where am I?'

Lucinda squeezed her hand. 'Home.'

Another breath hauled in. God, she was grateful for that taste of air. For a time there, she thought living was a thing of the past. The girl had dark rings around her eyes and her cheeks had lost some of their bloom. 'You okay?' Opi said in a weak voice.

Lucinda cracked a smile and sniffed. 'Yes. Finally one of you is awake.'

Opi was slow on the uptake. 'One of us?'

'Dad's still unconscious. Induced coma. A specialist is on the way. It's pretty bad.'

Tears threatened to spill over. Her eyes burned. There were no tears to cry. He lived. *Thank the bloody stars!* Opi tried to sit up, but found she couldn't. She was too weak. 'How long have I been out of it?'

'A week since we pulled you from the pod.'

Opi gaped at her. Tried to speak but the words only came on the second attempt. 'A week? Tell me everything.'

Lucinda screwed up her face. 'I can tell you what I know.'

'Go on.'

'Well, Rae and Essa are on their way.'

Opi lifted a hand, pointed a finger to the sky. 'Up there.'

Lucinda shifted in her seat. 'Oh.' She compressed her lips, then spoke. 'A second government ship came through the jumpgate. Double E said this one started picking up the ships that the first ship hadn't already destroyed. They also did a sweep for escape pods. The bad government ship that was chasing you and dad, got destroyed by our cannon on the moon. Your escape pod was blown into Islay 2's gravitational field and you fell here. The failsafe engaged, so while you had a bumpy ride, the chute's prevented a big...what did Double E say...oh yeah...splat.'

'That explains the headache.' She moved, an arm, a leg, her back. 'All over body ache.'

Lucinda, she noticed was excited about something. 'And something else has happened?'

Lucinda nearly bounced out of her seat. 'Yes!' She clapped her hands together. 'A new ship arrived this morning. The pilot said you ordered it. As he has family here, he's gone to visit them before a scheduled transport comes to collect him. He said the second ship was due next week. Did you order a new ship?'

'Must have.' Her memory was hazy and then she remembered putting through the order. 'I think it was because I was stealing your Dad's ship at the time.'

'But my dad was with you so you can't have stolen it, but it is gone.' She put her hands together then mimicked an explosion. 'Kaboom. Just like that. Dad loved *Matilda*. It's probably a good thing he's not awake...yet. He's going to be pissed about that.'

She laid her head on Opi's hand and without warning burst into tears.

Opi lifted her other hand, stroked the girl's hair. She was a lot like Rae. 'I'm sure he will be all right.'

Lucinda sat back and wiped her eyes with the back of her hand. 'I hope so. I'm sorry. I shouldn't have done that.'

Opi smiled wanly. 'Yes, you should have. You can cry on me anytime you feel inclined. If my head didn't hurt so much I'd do the same.' She tried to climb higher in the bed but found she couldn't. 'Can you give me a hand? I want to sit up a bit.'

Lucinda helped her move up the bed and found more pillows to support her, fluffing them before placing them. 'Thank you. Now tell me is there a doctor?'

'Yes, the doc is with dad at the moment. I'll let her know you want to see her. Can you eat something?'

'Yes, I can. Something light.'

***

The last spoonful of chicken soup had just been downed when an elderly woman walked in. She was dressed in serviceable grey coveralls. 'Oh good,' she said. 'Eating at last. You'll be out of that bed in no time at all. I'm Doctor Milberry. Sarah people usually call me.'

'Hi doctor. What can you tell me about Owain?'

The woman had long grey hair looped around her head and wrinkles seaming her face in comfortable lines. She parked her hip on the edge of the bed. 'My dear, I can give you the standard line. He's currently in cryo stasis awaiting the specialist.'

Opi's eyebrows rose. 'Cryo? He's that bad?'

'It was all I could do to hold him in life. Although once Dr Kumar arrives then we'll know more.'

'What is it burns, lacerations...brain damage?' Her fingers clenched the covers. It was all her fault. If only she'd been smarter in stealing the ship.

'There are some burns. Cuts. A few broken bones, concussion. It's the spine that is worrying me the most.'

'Holy shit.'

'You don't ask about your own injuries. They were not light.'

'I feel okay...now.' Opi winced and touched her temple where the kettle drum was beating nicely.

Dr Sarah nodded. 'Your right leg has healed nicely. I think the Smart repair will be complete by tomorrow. You should be able to walk on it. The swelling on your cervical spine has gone down so we will be able to stop the heaviest painkillers. The crack in your skull has healed nicely, the little haematoma behind it dissolved with medication. You're going to have to take it easy. At least, another week keeping quiet. No space fight. No stress.'

'That is easier said than done.'

'We informed your family. I believe they are on their way. You have time to recuperate.'

'I have a business empire to run.' And a serious need to find out what happened to those damn space pirates.

Dr Sarah squeezed her hand. 'Take it easy. That's all I'm asking. He'll need you there when he wakes up.'

Opi's eyes widened. 'Why do you say that?'

She shrugged. 'I knew his wife, Ms Gayens.'

'So, I'm not his wife. I'm not Belle McDevitt.'

'I know that. He knows that. He called your name before I put him under. Many times. His last thoughts were of you.'

Opi just stared at the woman. What could she say to that? She had held him close. Had dragged him into the pod, held him tight as the ship exploded around them. She was the last thing he saw. He was the last thing she remembered before waking up here. She was the reason his planet had been under threat. The reason he was injured. He would very likely call her name. He probably wanted to sue her for every penny he could get. That she looked like his dead wife was just another reason to run as far from him as she could.

She had made love with Owain McDevitt. She had not pledged her life to him. These people were crazy to expect anymore.

With a sigh, she sank back on her pillows. Dr Sarah patted her hand and stood up. 'I'll leave you to rest. You can get up tomorrow. I've scheduled a protein and vitamin boost for you this evening. You'll feel much better in the morning.'

'Thank you.' Opi closed her eyes. Sleep came and grabbed her. Oblivion for a short time was welcome.

***

The next morning, Lucinda was there helping her walk, if walk was the term to use for the hobbling that she did, to the kitchen. When they got there, Opi saw that Lucinda had laid out the table, with a single flower in a vase in the centre and pretty crockery. A coffee pot decorated with flowers sat by the place setting, steam and coffee fumes gently wafting out of the spout. 'This is lovely.'

'I wanted to celebrate you getting out of bed.'

Opi grimaced as she sat down. 'That's really kind of you. What's on the menu?'

'Waffles with maple syrup. Real maple syrup and cream.'

'Cream?'

'Yes. Don't tell Dr Sarah. She thinks cream is the root of all evil. However, it's my favourite thing and I'd like to share that with you.'

'I have a weakness for cream. Is it whipped?'

'Oh yes.' Lucinda returned with a plate, with two crispy waffles. Then she placed a jug of syrup and a big bowl of cream and a smaller dish of crushed pistachios.

Opi's stomach rumbled. 'Well now. You're going to join me aren't you?'

'You don't mind?'

'Of course not. You did all the work. You should enjoy it. Besides, we're friends aren't we?'

'Yes.' Lucinda made up a place for herself and together they demolished a goodly portion of the cream and syrup. Lucinda made a second batch of waffles.

Opi sat back in her chair and groaned. 'My god. I think I'm going to rupture something.'

Lucinda giggled. 'So Dr Sarah said you were to rest on the patio for at least an hour. Apparently sunlight is required to finish off your leg repair. Double E gave me a handheld for you. He said you should be able to restore yours from the backup in the house link and then VesperNet. Also, take this. It's got all kinds of books and movies on it.' Lucinda passed her a small entertainment unit.

'You've thought of everything.'

Lucinda got up and placed all the dirty utensils in the washer. Opi sat there waiting, observing the girl. Lucinda spun around and gaped at her. 'Oh I thought you'd gone.'

Opi swallowed. Not sure how Lucinda would react. 'Before I go outside, can I...can I see him?'

Lucinda broke eye contact and looked down. 'I don't think he'd want you to just now.' She looked up, gave a faint smile. 'He's very proud of who he is, resilient, dependable, handsome. I think he'd want you to see him whole and strong. Not like he is now all broken.'

Opi gazed at the girl. 'I agree that's what he would think. I need to see him, Lucinda. He doesn't need to know I did. I just need to know for myself that he's alive. You understand?'

Lucinda sniffed and wiped at a tear. 'All right. I'll take you to where he's on ice. I won't tell him, please don't tell him either.'

'I won't.'

Lucinda stayed at the door and let Opi pass through. The light was dim, but she heard the sounds of the unit. He wasn't quite frozen, more like his body had been taken to the edge and held there. A temporary thing until medical assistance could be arranged. He wasn't dead. The readouts told her than much and she closed her eyes and breathed in relief and guilt and something else. His body was inert but she remembered seeing him move. God, she remembered the feel of his skin on hers, the heat of him surrounding her, within her. It had been so good. Now it had come to this.

Red marks covered the right side of his chest. Burns. New skin had been grafted there. Swelling on his right temple. A leg braced with metal. Bruising around the eyes. Lips puffy and split. Hands swollen. Left forearm slightly out of shape.

Cataloguing his injuries kept her mind off her emotions, kept the grief in check. Would he live? She prayed that he would. Would he regain his full self? She wished she hadn't dragged him into this mess. Hadn't ruined everything. All because she'd said yes to a date in a restaurant. All because she liked his smile. Damn it. She was stupid. Look what she'd done to a perfectly nice man. She'd almost got his whole planet destroyed. She had to get away.

***

Lucinda left her alone while she sat in the sun on the patio. The mountains changed colour as she watched, the light smoothing planes and cloud shadows emphasising valleys. Why had McDevitt brought her here? Was he trying to break her heart?

The handheld quickly accessed her profile from backup and restored it. Everything was where it should be on VesperNet. Yet, it took three tries to get the retina scan to work. Her hands were that shaky. There was little news on the public channels about the space pirate battle. Damn, the government was keeping it under wraps. As much as she didn't want to, she switched to news of the space station attack. That would be harder to hide, given it was so public. She scanned the casualty lists from Space Station Beta C. Mueller was dead. She suspected his team was. Riley? His name wasn't on the list. Rani was gone. Pravi too. Ah shit…The pirates must have come back and cleaned up after themselves. Damn Polly. How could she?

There was no point in rebuilding her team. Not now. She'd just have to wing it on her own for the present. There was a private security company she could contract in when she got home, got back to Earth. Security was a necessary evil but she wasn't going to have an exec team again. Couldn't face it.

***

Three days later, she heard the scream of burning air and realised it was a ship coming into land.

'Double E?'

Her comm link chimed. Double E said, 'This lot is yours. I'll bring them over.'

Tears flooded her eyes. What the hell was wrong with her? Dr Sarah said she was bound to be emotional. Opi thought that was rot, but she couldn't deny she was stretched tight mentally. She'd been building for that battle. Thought that would be it. It was done. She just didn't know how done. She thought she'd be dead and she wasn't. That meant continuing on with plans. Senator Burr was in her sights for starters.

Chapter Fourteen

Families

Rae and Essa swarmed into the lounge where she was sitting with Lucinda. The young girl had been very attentive to her needs. Opi considered that Lucinda didn't want to be alone while her father was in such a state. It made sense. It did worry her that Lucinda was forming a bond with her. Mostly, Opi thought, because she was the spitting image of her mother.

After all the greetings were out of the way, Rae kept looking at Lucinda. 'I think I know you. You go to my school.'

Lucinda studied Rae, her eyes travelling all over her. 'Yes, you're in your final year, aren't you?'

Her gaze shifted to Essa. 'You're identical twins.'

Essa and Rae shared a look. They were both dressed differently. Essa had changed her hair. It was mostly shaved off and the rest dyed a lurid green. 'Yes. But you look like us, now that I think about it.'

Rae looked between Opi and Lucinda. 'Is there something you're not telling me?'

Opi sighed. Essa was watching all of them in turn. Maybe, she had figured it out.

Lucinda enlightened them. 'My mother and yours were twins too. I guess that makes me a sister or a cousin.' Her eyes were lively and she could hardly sit still.

Rae gaped at her, then pulled her head back as if eyeing some specimen. 'My mother is an only child.'

Essa sat forward. 'Another clone?'

Lucinda's expression dropped. 'Yes. A clone apparently, but my father said it was politer to call my mother a twin, she having equal rights as any other human being.' Lucinda stood up, her eyes a challenge, her hands curled to fists.

Essa waved her down, like she was putting out a fire. 'We get it. I'm a clone too.'

Opi objected. 'We call it a twin.'

Essa turned to Rae. 'Well, what do you think? Sister or cousin? I think she looks an awful lot like us.'

'She looks like Opi.' Rae sighed. 'I guess it has to be sister. Not that I need another one of those.'

Essa sighed theatrically and put hand to her waist in her trademark pose. 'Definitely. I need compensation. You were such a pain. I'm guessing this time though we won't have to share a dorm room with her. And technically she's a half-sister, not a twin so she won't be elbowing in on our turf.'

Lucinda's expression grew quite perturbed. She cast Opi a look and then studied Rae and Essa. They burst out laughing. Rae stretched out her open arms, wide smile on her face. 'Come here and give your big sisters a hug,' Rae said.

Lucinda grinned shyly and walked up to them. By the time they had finished hugging each other, Opi was teary and the girls were sniffing like crazy and dabbing their eyes.

Alwin walked in. 'What's the deal?' He waved to Opi. 'You okay Ms G?'

'Fine. I need to talk to you. I have some data I want you to dig through.'

'Freelance rates?' His dark eyebrow lifted. He caught her frown. 'Family discount?'

Opi shook her head. 'Where's Captain Thorn? I figured he's the one that brought you.'

'He's showing Double E over the new ship.' Essa said casually.

Rae lifted her head. 'You mean he's drooling over the new ship. Double E said you replaced one that got blown up. The new one is totally revved according to him. He says his boss will be pleased. Are you really sending him another one?'

Opi nodded. 'Yes, a backup. I put this planet at risk. I have to make sure they can defend themselves and evacuate if needed. The backup ship is quite a lot bigger than the old one. Dr Sarah reckons that it would be enough for all them in a pinch.'

'Evacuate?' All three girls said in unison.

'I'm not saying they have to evacuate, but just in case they ever need to. Risk management planning. Come on, haven't I taught you anything?'

Essa and Rae shared a look and turned sour expressions on Opi. Opi shook her head. They really weren't interested in the family business.

They progressed onto the patio and Lucinda organised a lot of food. The girl was quite resourceful. Although, she did rely on frozen catering packs for some of it. Opi couldn't help getting teary watching all three of her daughters prepare a meal together. They chatted non-stop, squealed, exclaimed. She heard Rae. 'You have a horse? No way.'

The situation ate at her insides. It contrasted what could have been with what was. Her clone might have lived. Yet, deep down it pleased her that Belle had met a good man, had a great life. Better than Vee had done. Better than Opi had done herself. Why did she have to go and think that?

Thorn came in, gave her a huge hug. 'Ma!'

She slapped his shoulder. 'Don't be cheeky.'

'But you are kinda my ma!'

'Essa doesn't even call me that. I feel like I need to be chewing straw or something. You may call me Ms G. Which I find annoying, but not exactly irritating, or Opi.'

Essa slid into Thorn's arms. 'Come over here. We have a new sister.'

Opi slid away and tucked herself into the deadroom. It wasn't long before Alwin came looking for her. He shut the door after him.

He put his feet on a low table and casually took in the room, nodding to himself as if he was impressed by what he saw. 'So fill me in.'

Opi told him about her plans. The layers of plans she had made and had kept mostly to herself. When she mentioned Polly and her betrayal he nearly leaped out of his seat.

'Polly? That social secretary air head?'

'Yes, her.' She described the scene with Mueller's head.

He paled. 'Good god. How did I miss it? I examined the history of all your team.'

'I don't think you missed it. I think she was suborned after your investigation.'

'But you were so close. That had to have hurt.'

'It did. I lost my team. Rani is dead. Pravi, my new bodyguard too according to the casualty reports. They were taken out on Space Station Beta C when the pirates attacked. Although I'm pretty sure Polly did the job herself. There was always a rivalry between her and Rani.'

'Rani had brains. That's why.' Alwin rubbed at the side of his head. 'So you say the government ship you called for backup started killing off the pirate ships and was coming after you.'

'Yes.'

'So your government contact was involved with the pirates?'

'I think so. Senator Burr. I've known him most of my life. He was the only one I told about my plan. He helped me get the two minnows and some contraband weapons that were on my ship, which was destroyed in the attack on Space Station Beta C. He was the one the minnows sent a code to signal the government ship to pick up the pirates for interrogation.'

'So you know he's a traitor and a criminal, what do you want from me?'

'I need the proof. Also, I need to know who sent for the second government ship. The one that picked up the pirates and has them hidden away.'

Alwin nodded, rubbed his chin. 'You know what the headlines are saying?'

'There were none when I looked a couple of days ago. I thought it must have been covered up.'

'Senator Burr issued a statement. He said that his operation had exterminated the entire space pirate operation.'

'That pig! His operation my ass!' Opi fidgeted on her seat.

Alwin wasn't done. 'He said he had some assistance from Ms Opeia Gayens, whose AllEarth Corp had been severely compromised through extensive pirate infiltration throughout her organisation.'

'He knows it went further than that. The government was infiltrated too.'

Alwin lifted an eyebrow as he delivered the last bit. 'He also said that he had run his own investigation and that the government was free of involvement in any pirate activity.'

'Damn him and blast. What a nasty piece of misinformation. See you have to find the proof!'

'I will get started. Where particularly?'

'You need to chase that ship that we destroyed. No, that won't work. I asked him to send it.'

'But you didn't give a kill order.'

'No, I didn't. I don't have the authority for that anyhow. They were to capture for later interrogation. You say he said all the pirates were destroyed, but they weren't. They were collected by the other government ship. Who sent the other ship? Where are the prisoners? Their interrogations should pin him too. Unless, they want to cover up the connection to the government, to the senator.' She shook her head and pursed her lips.

'Let's hope there isn't a cover up and that the information leads to him. Those prisoners have not surfaced anywhere yet. Not according the news headlines.'

Opi nodded. 'I need to remove Senator Burr from power. I need him prosecuted. How dare he take the credit for my operation? I risked my life to lure those pirates out. If it hadn't been for McDevitt I'd be dead.'

'This is Lucinda's father I take it.'

'Yes, damn him. I tried to keep him out of it but he kept being where he wasn't meant to be. Trying his macho bullshit, ordering me around.'

Alwin nodded. 'You don't like him then?'

'I didn't say that. He's a good pilot and a...' she shrugged. 'A good man. I wouldn't be alive if not for him.'

'I see...'

'No, you don't see. He was married to my clone. When he looks at me he sees her. He grows potatoes. I run a multi sector corporation.'

Alwin let out a sigh, examined her face and then climbed out of his seat. 'I'll get on this. Are we taking you home with us?'

'Yes. Do you mind waiting until the specialist gets here. I don't want to leave Lucinda alone while her father's condition is precarious. Once the specialist says he's in the clear, then I'll go.'

'Sure. I believe there's some horse riding planned. You okay with that?'

Opi laughed. 'As if I could stop them.' She rubbed her behind. 'I tried it already...and survived.'

Chapter Fifteen

Missing

Back on earth, things were a little interesting. Opi was fully recovered. Some journalists requested interviews which she refused. Her hired security guards weren't that efficient. A very audacious reporter, with a hover cam and mic, cornered her after she left a board meeting in AllEarth Towers.

'Is it true, Ms Gayens that you engineered the whole battle with the space pirates off Islay 2?' The woman's little feet scootered across the marble floor, trying to keep up.

Opi tried to dodge around her. 'I told you I have no comment.' Secretly she was annoyed. That reporter must have done some digging to get that angle on the story or someone on Islay 2 had leaked information.

'Is it true you were willing to sacrifice your own life to destroy those nasty space pirates?'

'No comment.'

'Is it true that you nearly died?' The woman stood in front of her blocked her path, tried to get nose to nose with mic in-between.

Opi had to stop and face the woman. The reporter's spikey dark brown hair looked stiff and uncomfortable. Her clothing was all black leather and buckles. She looked all of twenty years old.

'No comment.'

The report groaned. 'Come on, give me a break here. Please.'

Opi paused, a mistake. The reported darted in front of her again. 'Is it true that your life was saved by an undercover military man, one Owain McDevitt?'

That stopped her. 'Where did you hear that?'

'Earth Security released statement not one hour ago.'

'Is McDevitt all right?'

The reporter's eyes widened. 'His condition is unknown at this stage.'

Opi nodded, hoping she hadn't revealed too much. 'Thank you. Good day.' She signalled to her security guards and they formed up around her and the pesky reporter who had so shaken her was squeezed out of the way.

It had been six goddamn weeks.

Why hadn't she heard from him? Had he been blocked? It took her several days for her to review her daily correspondence. With no exec team, she had to do it herself. Yet, there had been nothing from McDevitt. His name was on the priority list. No news. Nothing from Islay 2. Surely even common courtesy would dictate a short get well note. She'd sent him one.

Fear punched her hard in the gut. What if? No, she didn't want to think that, or believe that. She recorded another message to send to Islay 2, leaving it open so anyone could read it. Just in case McDevitt hadn't recovered. Tears threatened and she pushed them angrily away. The temptation to go off planet and visit Islay 2 was strong.

The comms chimed and she jumped. Dayton's face appeared on screen. 'It is good to see you looking so well.' He commented with a finger salute to her.

'You mean you're glad I'm not looking dead.'

He nodded. 'That would have been inconvenient at this stage. I would have been left holding the bag so to speak.' He lifted his chin. 'You saw my report?'

'Yes. I'm not quite ready for the final tranche to go yet. I have some unfinished business. Just one more piece.'

'Understood. Just give the word. Everything is in readiness. And just in case I don't get the chance to speak to you again, let me say how much I enjoyed working with you. My bank account has surely benefited.'

'Thank you for being so efficient.'

By the end of the week, a message had arrived from Islay 2. She keyed it up. Double E's image appeared on screen. 'Ms Gayens. Thank you for your message. I am glad to see that you were well when your message was dispatched. Lucinda sends her regards. Unfortunately, she has returned to school and is not here at the moment. I am unable to give you word of McDevitt. He was revived and had his injuries treated before he left. He didn't tell me where he was going. If you hear from him please ask him to contact me.

'By the way, the second ship has arrived. Oh my god! Ms Gayens it is a beauty. We are still going over it, but my word the specs are amazing. Why the sick bay is better equipped than our own med centre. Dr Sarah said to tell you it was ace and that she may use if for a clinic when it is not in being flown.'

Opi smiled and then sighed. Where the hell was McDevitt? He had been undercover. Was he still working for the security forces? Was it him that sent for the second government ship? No. She thought he would have said. Her mouth squished up as she considered this, then she remembered that pulling faces would give her more wrinkles so she smoothed her expression.

The fallout from the security forces press statement created a media frenzy. Her comms link had to be disconnected. Senator Burr had been asked to provide a new statement in Parliament. The President was initiating a wide ranging inquiry into Senator Burr's activities. Opi's heart leapt. One last piece.

Taking a number of steadying breaths, she dialled up Burr's office. His assistant answered the call. He was bound to be inundated but she had access to his private line.

'The senator will call you back shortly, Ms Gayens.'

Opi took time to check that her hair and that her beige pantsuit was immaculate and totally corporate chic. She must not appear rattled. Although, intellectually she could see the evidence pointed to Burr, emotionally it was hard. He'd been her supporter in the early days. A friend when she'd had trouble with Carl and when he'd gone to prison. He'd called her personally when Carl had died. A lot of water had gone under that bridge.

'Opeia, how nice of you to call. How good to see that you escaped harm on your little escapade.'

'Thank you. That news report was not sourced from me. I want you to know that.'

Burr's eyebrows drew together in thought. 'You saw my earlier press release?' He shrugged. 'Politics. You know how it is. Positive spin and all that.'

'I understand. I have no wish to make my part of the story widely known. Only that AllEarth Corp is finally free of corruption.'

His eyebrows shot together above serious eyes. 'A government cruiser was destroyed. I had to account for it. I sent it as per our agreement.'

Opeia put a hand to her head, feigning a headache 'I'm sorry. My injuries still trouble me. I believe the cruiser did not quite obey orders.'

His smile was half articulated. 'Yes, well it was a dangerous move you took there. It's very hard to control a battle from a distance. Friendly fire and all that.'

'Yes, very friendly.'

He picked up his handheld. 'Oh well, if that is all.' His eyes lifted to hers. 'Was there a problem? Some other issue you wished to raise?'

Opi studied him for a moment. 'No. Nothing. I just wanted to thank you and wish you well.'

'You're welcome. Perhaps I'll see you at the Clages' Cocktail Party next week.'

'Perhaps. One thing before you go.'

He lifted his head, not quite meeting her eye. 'Yes?'

'I seem to be missing someone.'

His smile widened and then he lifted his head so he was looking directly at her. 'Who?'

Opi played it carefully. No direct accusations. 'I'm not sure if you can help me. Have you heard of Owain McDevitt?'

'Ah yes… that name is familiar.' He used a finger to change screens on his handheld. 'Here it is. A little bird told me you went on a date.' He grinned at her and winked. 'Romance at your age. Mmm…McDevitt. Yes, that was the name of the fellow.' He grinned and it wasn't nice. 'Did he show you a good time?'

Opi wanted to punch him in his smug face. 'Our date was a little interrupted by a pirate attack.'

He nodded, mouth creased in a sour expression. 'Romantic attachments, Opeia? I had thought that you…well that your interests didn't lie in that direction.'

'I'm not romantically attached to anyone.'

He dropped the handheld onto the table. 'Oh. I'm sorry to hear that. I had heard that he was rather taken with you. Seems you and his wife shared something. A close bond.'

Her fists clenched. The bastard knew too much. He must have been investigating her as hard as she was investigating him. 'He has your genetic daughter, too. How awkward for you. To be nothing but the shadow of his long, lost wife. Carl did you over well didn't he? You have my sympathies as always.'

Opi couldn't believe she'd fallen for his smarmy ways previously. What an idiot she had been. Arranging a pleasant expression on her face, she replied. 'I believe Belle McDevitt had a wonderful life despite Carl Gayens. That much pleases me. What's your point?'

'You brought it up, dear. I don't know where your McDevitt is.' He picked up his handheld again, flicking screens quickly. Then he looked into the viewer. 'I know where the child is though. I know how much your DNA matters to you.'

'It does. What do you want?' Damn him. She'd have to get in touch with the school, arrange security.

'Thanks to you, my dear. I have an image problem. I expect you to be at the cocktail party next week and my campaign manager will be in contact with you shortly. We think you can help us out, support my re-election campaign.'

Opi leant back and bit her bottom lip. 'Sure. While I'm head of AllEarth Corp I'll be your supporter.'

'Make sure you are.' He keyed off.

Opi growled at her viewscreen. That bastard knows something. Where was McDevitt? Did Burr have him? She keyed up her comms link. 'Al? What have you got for me? Burr just threatened Lucinda.'

'I don't have much yet. It's coming together. I have something from Polly's journal. She recorded notes of her meetings. I just need to break the code.'

'Any word on where those prisoners are? The security forces made a statement. All hell is breaking lose. McDevitt is missing.'

'Missing? What do you mean?'

'I heard from Islay 2. Double E said he'd left the planet but didn't say where he was going.'

'Did he take the new ship?'

'I didn't ask. Maybe, why?'

'I think I can contact him if he's on that ship. It has a code. If he's on it and conscious he'll answer.'

Opi closed her eyes. 'I hope so. I just need to know he's okay, you know. That Burr doesn't have him stashed somewhere. Let him know I'm keeping an eye out for Lucinda.'

'I will. I'll get back to you.'

'You do that.' Opi sat back in her chair and rubbed at her temples. She didn't have to feign a headache. She had one, ripe and bursting. She fumbled for some pain killers and went to lie down.

***

When Alwin called back he didn't have good news. 'No response.'

'Can you tell where the ship is?'

He shook his head. 'Not unless I search all docking ports in the sector.'

'What about Burr?'

Alwin shook his head. 'Nothing concrete yet. You?'

'No word from anybody. I'm going to take Lucinda out for the day. She has a free pass from school.'

'Be careful.'

'I am. Gris has been keeping an eye on her.'

'Gris? Yes, he will be good for her. Particularly while Rae is with me. I heard he and Vee are getting close.'

'Really? I hadn't heard that. I hope it works out for them.' Her damaged clone deserved something good in her life.

Opi's headache was still hanging around, but she worked fast to get through her workload so she could make the date with Lucinda.

While they were sitting in a mall café, after some impressive shopping, Opi listened to Lucinda talk about school, her worries. Her heart was touched at how accepting Lucinda was of her. She had to put away her paranoia that she was a replacement for Belle. Something that stuck in her craw. She was used to thinking clones were shadows of her and not the other way around. That made her get angry at herself for it revealed a prejudice that she didn't think she had. Again, knowing Belle had had a good life, married, loved and produced a daughter all on her own made Opi feel superfluous. If she truly believed that clones had equal rights what was her problem? That this particular clone did all right without any help from her? With a sigh, she nodded to Lucinda and took a sip of her coffee.

There was a commotion out in the main part of the mall. Something caught her eye. She stiffened. 'Gris?'

The old retainer, a long-time friend and protector of Rae's, nodded and went out to check.

'Hurry up with your drink, Lu. I think it's time we were heading back.'

'Oh?' she finished off her milk shake. 'All done.'

Gris showed his face at the door, a quick nod, confirming there was trouble. 'Okay. We're off.'

'What's that noise?'

'I don't know.' She put her hand on Lucinda's back. 'I don't want to find out either.' She turned to their protector. 'Gris?'

'I've called for backup, Ma'am.'

'What is it?' Lucinda asked, voice rising with panic.

Then Opi saw them. A gang of men and women. Not the usual sort. They weren't bothering with people other than shoving them out of the way. They were headed directly for them.

'Gris, I think we'd better run. Where is mall security? The security droids?'

'They aren't responding.'

'Right.'

Opi had been working on her fitness but it wasn't quite pre escape pod levels. Lucinda was quick of foot. While the crease between her brows indicated she didn't understand, she didn't argue.

Opi put her hand in her purse and then ducked around the corner. 'Gris. Take Lucinda back to school.'

'No!' Lucinda cried out. 'I'm not leaving you.'

'Gris,' she repeated.

'Sorry, Ma'am. Can't leave you alone.'

'Damn it to hell. Do it your way.'

She peeked around the corner and the gang was still coming, not running but walking swiftly and with a purpose. Pulling back, she rechecked the charge on her weapon. It was licensed for stun. She hoped it would be enough.

Popping her head out again, she called out a warning. 'Back off or I'll fire.'

Not even a check in their step. 'Bugger!' She leant out and squeezed off a shot.

She hit two of them and they fell to the ground, quivering bodies, heels banging against the floor. Another quick peek and the rest were still coming. Not even stopping to check on their fellows. She fired again. Hit three this time before a shot exploded above her head, flinging concrete chips over her and onto the floor.

Unregistered projectile weapon, she was pretty sure. This time she lay flat and pushed herself out. They were so close. She got the lead, the one with the gun. And the two behind. Their numbers were thinning out. A woman, all tattoos and denim, picked up the projectile weapon and raised it. Opi downed her and the one behind. The last two, seeing their mates all convulsing or unconscious on the floor, turned and fled.

Gris dragged her to her feet. 'You took too much of a chance, Ma'am. Rae wouldn't like that.'

'Yes, I know, but now let's leave. Call the transport. I want to be picked up at the door.'

Gris spoke into his comms link and then checking their surroundings went on their way. Sirens started blaring and security droids could be heard droning.

That was all very convenient. There was a silent hand at play here and she had a pretty good idea whose that was. That meant that he did have an eye on Lucinda and probably her too.

'Lucinda,' she said when they climbed in the car. 'I'm going to drop you back at school. But if there is any trouble, any reason you feel unsafe, you tag, Gris, okay? He'll bring you to me. I'd take you home with me now but I don't have your dad's permission for an overnighter.'

'Sure.' Her eyebrows lowered. 'What was all that about? Why did you have a weapon? Is it always like this for you?'

'Not always. The weapon is a precaution. That's the first time I've had to use it ever. What do you think? Good shot or what?'

'Not bad. Scary though. You only stunned them so I suppose they'll be okay.'

'Yes, just stun. Nasty headache when they come to.'

'Why did they come after you? How did they know where you were?'

Opi looked out the window, watched the traffic pass them by. Saw the police arriving at the mall. They'd be in contact. It was all on the surveillance camera. Normally she'd have Polly deal with them, but she'd have to do it herself. Despite Polly betraying her, she missed her. They'd been friends and Polly had been efficient too.

She cast Lucinda a look. 'I had a gut feeling. There's stuff going on. It made sense.'

'Stuff like the battle in Islay 2's system?'

'Yes. Did your dad explain?'

'Not much. He thinks I don't get it. But it's why he left. He went off in that new ship, *Matilda 2*. Said he had some business to finish.'

'That's good to know. Did he say where he was going? When he'd be back?'

'No. Just said he'd see me when school was over as usual.'

'Right.'

'Gris. Did that additional security report in?' Opi had noted two cars, one behind and one flanking her.

'Yes, Ma'am. They have joined us.'

'Good. Then can you accompany Lucinda back to school and stand by in case she needs you?'

'Yes Ma'am. I know the drill.'

***

As much as she hated the idea, Opi went to the cocktail party. She hated every minute of it. Disillusionment and anger were fuelling her new view of the world. Most of the people in the room were known to her, but none of them were friends. It was all about who had what and how to get it out of them. It hadn't bothered her in the past. It was how things were. Now she knew things could be different. And she knew Burr was crooked. She just had to prove it.

Burr came up to her. 'Opeia darling. You came. How good of you to spare the time.' He air kissed both sides of her cheeks.

A media bot hovered and he grabbed her to him for a pose. 'The pleasure is all mine,' Opeia said for the camera.

'Where's McDevitt?' she whispered urgently in his ear.

'Love sick are we? Well, he must be good in bed to have you panting after him.'

They clinked glasses. 'You're a sick bastard, you know that? McDevitt is an innocent bystander in this. You've got no business...'

'McDevitt is not an innocent bystander. Didn't you know he works for Earth security? Why don't you ask them instead of blaming me?'

'Then you don't have him?'

He smiled at her, but the look in his eyes chilled her. 'Now that would be telling and I know absolutely nothing about anything...'

He leant in close and said through clenched teeth. 'Stop digging.'

She smiled thinly. 'Me? I know absolutely nothing about anything.' She threw his line back at him. Just then they were interrupted by a mutual acquaintance.

Opi stayed as shorter time as she could get away with and then slipped away.

She keyed up her comms link. 'Alwin? Tell me you have some news.'

'I'm at your place. Where are you?'

'Not five minutes away.' She shut off her link and frowned in the back seat of her transport. The city flowing by in a blur.

Heart beating double time, Opi raced to her door and keyed the lock.

'Al?'

'In here.'

He was at her workstation and had a cold beer by his side. His dark eyes met hers when she walked in. 'Found your missing pirates.'

'Where are they?'

'Earth security has them on an off-world facility. Not a space station. Looks like Europa.'

'Good. So they are alive. Any news on the interrogations? Confessions? Connections?'

'No. They are being interrogated but they have the information locked up tight. You'll have to ask.'

'What about McDevitt? I'm worried about him.'

Alwin nodded. 'So this guy you dated was undercover right?'

'He said so.'

'You didn't believe him?'

'Well, not really. It seemed weird that I was running this operation with the government's knowledge and that they were running another one that I didn't know about. Seems damned inefficient to me.'

'But if they suspected your operation of being infiltrated? Wouldn't it make sense to keep something back from you?'

Pouting, she tugged at her bottom lip. 'I suppose so. A bit insulting if you ask me.'

'The Burr connection?'

'I didn't know about him then and I don't think they did either. So if McDevitt was undercover, really undercover with Earth Security, then he was probably the one with the pull to call that other government cruiser and probably why no one has quizzed me about the destruction of the other one. *The Runaway*. Although Burr did say he had to answer questions.'

'That ship's crew mostly escaped. There were some deaths but most of the crew made it to escape pods and were picked up by the other ship. It appears they are being interrogated too.'

'I hope one of them can point to Burr.'

'So, do you think McDevitt was behind that press release? It seemed to depict what went on pretty accurately. "Ms Opeia Gayens battles the space pirates. Rae jumps up and down every time she sees the headlines.'

Opi smiled. 'She would. I'm trying to keep a low profile here and run a multi-sector corporation. It might have been Earth Security and not McDevitt. He's gone to ground or has been taken out of commission.'

'You need to put your team on it.' Al covered his mouth and looked around the room meaningfully. 'You have no team.'

Opi's face fell. Al sat forward and lifted a hand. 'Sorry. I shouldn't have said that. You can't bring yourself to hire a new crew can you?'

Opi shook her head. 'No. Not at the moment. It's too fresh, too painful. I'm coping.'

'Sure you are.' Al nodded. 'Well then, back to McDevitt. I've tracked *Matilda 2* to guess where, Space Station Beta C.'

Opi lowered her eyebrows. 'Beta C? What would he be doing there?'

'Can't say, but station records say the ship has been there for a month and there's been no sighting of McDevitt. He's disappeared.'

Heart thumping, Opi seized on this information. 'Burr has him. I've just got to get McDevitt out of this.'

'Send in station security,' Alwin suggested.

'And say what? That's a big station. Look, go over the specs for me. See if there is somewhere someone could be stashed or hidden away.'

'I'm on it. I'll send the information through to your handheld.' He swung around in his chair, calling up the space station plans. 'What are you planning?'

'Never you mind. This is my business. You do your bit.'

He mock saluted her and went back to his screen.

Chapter Sixteen

Daring Do

Not having an exec team proved to have some advantages. Alwin had come up with three areas on Space Station Beta C where McDevitt could be held. Now, Opi could plan the rescue without having a team interfering and trying to protect her or direct her or tell how it should be done and how she might get hurt.

She hadn't counted on Alwin Anton interfering though, even though he was useful. He looked up from his handheld. 'Mrs G?'

'What?' Opi responded innocently.

'Belle McDevitt's identification?'

Opi tried for nonchalance and failed. 'Yes. Just for one week. Change the record to hide her death and then put the information back after seven days. After than it won't matter.'

'Just what are you planning?'

Opi didn't answer and sent through another request. He turned his gaze to his screen. 'Security pass. Mmm.'

He swung around in his chair again. 'Opi are you sure about this?'

She rested her chin on her hand, leaning her elbow on the desk. 'Yes. Can you keep quiet about it?'

'Why seven days?'

'I have to be back for Senator Burr's campaign launch. If I can keep up the pretext that I'm here he won't suspect. Using Belle McDevitt's ID allows me to go to the space station and not raise flags. The security pass will get me into places. Make sure I can destroy it if I'm captured. You can pretend to be me while I'm gone. I'll have a bunch of predetermined messages you can send out.'

Alwin nodded. 'All right. I can do that but I'm not happy about it. I should go with you.'

'No. I don't want you or the girls involved.' Opi opened a box that had been delivered. She grinned when she saw the bright yellow mouldable explosive with the DNA trigger. Who knew you could get multiple colours. She slid the packet into her shoulder bag. That was going with her.

Alwin shook his head. 'Rae will kill me if I keep it from her.'

'Just a week, Al. Tell her what you want after that.'

'Thorn could fly you.'

'No, I'm taking an express public transport. It's quick and anonymous. Make sure *Matilda 2* has no outstanding dock charges and is cleared for launch. I'll be bringing it back.'

'You really care for this guy don't you?'

Opi looked up and cocked her head. 'That's not why I'm doing this. He got caught up in something of my making. I have to make it right.'

'What if he's dead?'

Opi's expression froze. 'He can't be dead.'

Al grinned and then nodded slowly. 'I'll have this stuff ready in half an hour.' He pointed to her box of explosives. 'What's that?'

'A little something that might be useful. It is inert. When I touch it, it will code to my DNA and while I keep touching it, it will stay inert. I can shape it, pull it apart. As soon as I stop touching it once it's keyed to me, a chemical reaction starts. At first it sweats as each molecule checks for my DNA and doesn't find it, then the reaction starts. Depending on the coding, it takes about ten to thirty minutes, then it blows.' She tapped her bag. 'This one takes ten minutes to react.'

Alwin frowned at it. 'Nasty. But clever.'

'I thought so.'

***

The corridor was empty. Opi relaxed her shoulders and replaced her black market stunner into its holster. She'd been on the space station for one day. The first place she looked for McDevitt drew a blank. He hadn't been in the lock up. Too obvious. Now she had to get through security into the cryo holds. It was used for food, but Alwin's analysis suggested it would be a good hiding spot for a human cryo unit.

Straightening up, she marched down the corridor. Dressed in a black, tight-fitting body suit, she looked like security. Her pass swung from her belt. The security footage, if monitored, wouldn't be alerted by her presence. She did her best to move in a regimented fashion, like she was meant to be there. She paused at the entrance to each locker and tested the lock. This was her cover. The one she was looking to infiltrate was the main one at the end of the corridor.

Her pass let her in. The door lock flashed green and slid open. It was dark inside. A tall hanger with dark crates in stacks and the hum of machinery in the air. It held no particular nooks and crannies but did have lots of machinery. It was very well ordered and it didn't take long to check.

The first bay she inspected held freezer crates of meat carcases. So the *Hotel Magnifique* did use real meat after all. Walking along the rows of crates, she was on the lookout for something different. She doubted McDevitt would be in a meat crate. That kind of freezing would kill him. If he'd been iced, he'd be in a specialised unit. Otherwise they just would have killed him outright. That thought sent a shiver up her spine.

The more she looked around, the more convinced she was that he was here. It wasn't an obvious place to store a cryo unit, but she had a feeling and kept looking. In a cornered off section, she found what she'd been looking for. A sealed section with glass panels and when she pressed her nose up to the glass, there was a large cryo unit inside. Different from the freezer units. It had to be him.

Her security pass wasn't going to work on the sealed section. It had a manual lock. Lifting her head, she looked for security cameras and saw none. Letting out a breath, she reached into her pouch and took out the bright yellow plastic explosive. Using her teeth, she tugged off her glove and started massaging a small bit, while she assessed the door. The plastic explosive was so soft, it was pleasurable to squeeze, then finding what she thought was the right spot, she rolled the explosive into a sausage and pressed it along the door seal. Then she hunkered behind some meat crates and was cloaked in shadow. Time ticked by slowly. Ten minutes had never been so long.

The door blew with a soft whoosh. Opi blinked. She expected more somehow. Waving the smoke out of her face, she crept into the room. There was a cryo unit. She wiped the debris from the viewport and her heart fluttered. It was Owain. She crawled along the ground checking the readouts and trying to work out if she could move him, or whether it was safe to defrost him. The readout indicated that he was ready for defrosting, well, revival. She hit the button and hoped for the best.

An alarm blared overhead. She started, shocked by the suddenness of it and the pitch, tuned to make one want to run. Heart racing, she went to the door she'd just blown and took a peek out into the wider vault. The fumes from the explosion had triggered the alarm. While she looked on, security arrived. Six armoured security guards, with shields and some kind of weapon. Couldn't be projectile. Not in a space station environment. Laser or stunner. Neither good news.

Pulling back, she rested her head against the wall, eyeing McDevitt's cryo unit. 'Damn,' she said and kicked the metal box. It moved. She pushed at it with her toe. It moved again. It was on a maglev conveyer unit. That might work, provided McDevitt didn't pop out like a jack in the box at the wrong moment.

Drawing her stunner, Opi got behind the cryo unit and pushed, aiming for the door. The nozzle of her stunner lay along the top ready to fire as her targets came into view. If they avoided stun with their shields, well she'd just have to run them over.

A shot buzzed over her head, almost parting her hair. She sighted along the finder and squeezed off a shot. She caught the guard on the knee, just below where his shield protected him. He fell sideways, dropping the shield. Another shot and he was out of it. The cryo unit cleared the sealed room area and she was out in the open. A quick glance to the side and she saved herself some grief. She shot a security guard who had tried to outflank her. He went down in a tumble limbs and nervous tremors. Quickly as she could she shot off blind to the other side then swung around to the front, downing another one. There were three guards between her and the door.

Hopefully the corridor wasn't filling with backup troops. Her mind started thinking up plan Bs and Cs. Hiding out until McDevitt revived? Too risky. Besides then he'd want to save her and that wasn't how this operation was going down. It was her rescue.

One of the guards put his hand to his helmet, looking to be calling security control. Damn it, she couldn't have that. She shot him in the head before the other guards could react. She took them out too as they dropped their shields when they turned to see what happened to their fallen buddy.

Steering clear of the stunned guards, she made for the door. It was sealed up tight. She swiped her security pass and nothing happened. She tried it again. They had figured it out. There was no time to blow the door with her DNA plastic explosive as the guards would start getting control of their limbs back. She looked at her weapon. Not enough juice in it to blow the lock. Nothing else she had was good enough for the job.

Then she looked at one of the fallen guards. Now, they would have something. A quick search revealed a laser. That would fry circuits as well as flesh.

The door slid open and she took a peek down the corridor, careful to pull back in case someone took a shot. No one there yet. She targeted the security feed with the stolen laser. *Boom. Boom.* The cameras were gone.

Behind the cryo unit again, she pushed it out the door and promptly crashed it into the far side of the corridor. It wasn't as easy or as manoeuvrable as it looked. Finally, she righted the thing, pushing hard as she ran it down the long corridor. Now where to hide until the heat died down? She couldn't very well push the thing to the docking port and board *Matilda 2*.

She screwed up her face, realising she hadn't thought out her escape plan well. There was no hope for it, she would have to go to the next place she was going to look for McDevitt. It was a good hiding place at least. The cryo unit was a machine after all and where better to store one that in the spare parts storage bay. Some of those spare parts were quite big.

The service elevator came when she called it, using her Belle McDevitt ID. Why she did not know. The elevator was not secured. That meant that security had not flagged a wider issue. Yet.

There was traffic in the corridor as she exited to the spare parts bay. She was pushing a large metal container and no one appeared to bat an eyelid. So far so good. The main hatch was open and the guard there gave her a once over. 'What's that?'

'A cryo unit returning to store. I was sent down with it. Can you tell me where to put it?'

He shook his head and rolled his eyes. Thankfully, he didn't look to see if it was empty or not. He checked the storage bay map. 'Put it in 3C with the rest of them.' He held out a scanner for her ID. She tried her Belle McDevitt ID and it worked okay. No flags. Al must have given the ID wider security access than she expected. Good one. She'd send him a bonus if she got out of here.

Once in the area of 3C she looked for a place to hide out while McDevitt went through his revival cycle. The units were stored five high on purpose-built racks. She nestled behind a rack closest to the wall. It would give them enough privacy. She checked the face plate. McDevitt was still unconscious and then she crawled along the floor again to check the readouts. It had ten minutes to run. An orange light was blinking. Squinting at the label, she realised it was the power levels. She searched the racks for a power cell or cord. In the corner she found a large cupboard and inside was a set of cords.

A foot step sounded behind her. 'You finished yet?'

It was the guard who'd let her in. Blinking rapidly, she stalled as she thought of something. 'I have to plug the unit in so it can finish the clean cycle. Apparently, it didn't complete because they wanted to get rid of it. They needed the room.'

She waved the cord. He nodded. 'Okay then. Don't be too long. I'm going off shift. I'll let my replacement know you are still here. Wouldn't want you locked in. We seal up for night shift.'

'Sure, won't be long.' She shook her head. His boots clunked across the metal decking of the storage bay. She let out a breath. That was too close.

The cord inserted in the end and luckily there was a power outlet on the wall close enough to reach. She pushed the unit closer in and then looked around for a place to hide. The night duty guard was likely to come looking for her if he checked the sit rep reports and saw that she hadn't signed out. There was no help for it. She had to hide in a spare unit. Taking out her handheld, she set the timer. She didn't want McDevitt waking up alone.

The lid of the cryo unit was ajar and through the slit she saw a guard. He looked around, checked down the lanes of the racks and shook his head. Then he walked away. Phew! He thought she'd gone. Fingers crossed.

Next, she climbed back out and went to McDevitt's unit. A light flashed on the door release and she punched it. There was a crackle of electricity and the lid opened. McDevitt sucked in a breath, a halting, just punched in the gut breath, the one that didn't seem to fill the lungs. She grabbed his hand and squeezed. 'Relax. Breathe. You've been in cryo.' Her voice was pitched low. She hoped it penetrated the cryo haze. His next breath was a loud whoop, the next deep but entering normal space. His body tense, began to relax. Before she knew it the blue eyes were gazing at her in puzzlement, then looked behind her to the surroundings.

'Opi?'

He looked down. He wore only a white wrap around his hips. Nothing else. She hadn't thought of that. She had nothing to give him. That was going to make things awkward. Streaking naked through Beta C was a good way to draw security's attention.

She pushed the lid open and helped him step free. Then because it might retain their cover, she set the unit on clean and led him to the shadows behind the rack and checked him over.

He was still quite placid, probably a drug that the unit fed him to help him adjust. She ran her hands over his chest, his back. There was no sign of new trauma. A slight ridge on the skin of his chest was evidence of his previous skin graft. Her relief was such that she laid her face against his chest and sighed. 'You're okay.'

His hand came around her shoulders. 'Opi? What's going on?'

'I'm so glad you're all right.'

He gazed down at her and frowned. 'You didn't hang around. You didn't wait for me.'

The hurt look on his face, wounded her. 'I waited until you were on the mend. I had to do stuff.'

'Then why are you here?'

'You went missing. I figured Burr had you so I came looking.' She looked him up and down. His state of undress was very distracting. 'And I've found you. I've come to rescue you.'

The puzzled frown grew deeper then he shut his eyes and rubbed his forehead. Post cryo headache. It probably wasn't good for a man to have two cryo stints so close together.

Nestled there, she waited patiently. He had to be fully recovered before they made a move. She bit her bottom lip as she thought about where to get him some clothes.

'I remember I had an urgent message to meet you here on Space Station Beta C. I came but the rest is a blur.'

'I didn't send you a message. It was a trap. Senator Burr threatened Lucinda too. That's when I was sure he had you. Double E said you'd left and he didn't know where you were. You've been in cryo for a month.'

'A month? Why?'

'Leverage. Senator Burr is holding you over my head so I'll support his re-election campaign. I have to get back to Earth before he figures out I've set you free.'

'And Earth Security?'

She shook her head. 'They released a few press statements. I thought they came from you.' She lowered her gaze. 'When you didn't call me...well.'

'Mmm...' he said, running fingers through his hair. His chin had a short growth of beard. His body though was very warm.

'Wait here. I'm going to see if I can find you some clothes.'

After a few steps, she looked behind and saw that he still sat there, looking around him, his eyebrows arrowed together in concentration. He'd be all right alone for a few moments.

The storage bay appeared deserted. While it was a spare part storage bay she figured there must be a uniform around here, in a personal locker or in a dispenser. Right on the money. There were a stack of clean uniforms at the end of a slide chute. She rummaged through them looking for ones that would fit McDevitt. Unfortunately, there were no boots or shoes.

When she arrived back with the uniforms, McDevitt was more himself. He tugged the clothes from her hands and started dressing himself in quick movements. Opi looked and liked what she saw until McDevitt glanced at her. 'Do you mind?'

Opi took that as a rejection and turned away, cheeks burning in mortification. Fully dressed, except for shoes, he asked. 'Weapons?'

She showed him her stunner, partly discharged and the laser also part empty. He stood, did a double take of her and took the laser. 'The ship?'

'In dock and cleared for launch. Provided no one was left on station to keep an eye on you, we should make a clean break.'

He grunted and moved ahead of her to peek down the row between 3C and 3D. He waved for her to follow and she did. She was tempted to grumble, because he'd done that take over thing. He hadn't even said thank you.

The guard who was meant to be on duty was nowhere around. That was rather odd. 'Wait!' she cried, as McDevitt went to key open the main door.

'What?'

'No guard.'

He cocked his head.

'There should be a night guard. Something is wrong.' She pointed down the wall a way where there was a smaller door with an emergency exit sign over the top. 'Maybe it would be more discreet.'

He gave her a nod like a salute and changed direction. Before opening the door he assessed it. What he was checking the door for she wasn't sure. After a quick glance at her face, he said, 'Alarm.'

He was right. The door was wired. If they went that way they wouldn't be sneaking out. 'What about security feed?'

McDevitt shot his gaze around and then nodded toward a small office. They crept over there, keeping an eye on the main door. McDevitt sat himself down in the chair and called up the screens. Outside the main door was a squad of security types, weapons at the ready. Opi frowned and chewed her lips. How did they know? Then when she ran through the last hour or so she realised it was either the explosion or the opening of the cryo unit. Her bet was the cryo unit. Someone here was in the pay of Burr to keep McDevitt quiet.

McDevitt looked at another control panel. 'This controls the emergency doors. I think if I punch this, it will go to standby.'

Opi nodded. 'How long?'

McDevitt shook his head. 'Not sure, but at least that corridor is not full of troops.'

They left the small office and ran to the emergency exit.

She put her arm on McDevitt's. 'Wait. We need a diversion.'

His dark brows arrowed together. 'What diversion?'

Her hands were already kneading the explosive. 'Give me ten.'

Opi didn't want to hurt anyone, but she did want a distraction. She placed the explosive around the main door, to one side. It should keep the guards there. At first to control the explosion and next waiting to come through to pursue them.

Then she raced back to McDevitt and nodded. No audible alarms sounded when the pushed it open. After that they didn't care. The explosion went off. Alarms blared. Fumes surged up the corridor.

Their way out wasn't far from where the squad waited for them to exit through the main door. She leant around the corner to peak at them. They were definitely otherwise occupied, putting out the fire and some getting ready to deploy inside the storage bay.

McDevitt grabbed her by the arm and pulled her back. He pointed up to a cover of a ventilation shaft. Opi sagged. Not another access chute.

With a leg up, she was able to push the cover up and away. Then in the second attempt, McDevitt gave her a shove that sent her flying up assisted by low gravity. She lay flat against the floor of the access chute and leant down to give him a hand up. With an economical jump, he was up and then she edged away so he could use his elbows to lever himself inside. Carefully, he put the vent cover back.

'This way,' he whispered. They carefully crawled until the next junction. So far there were no signs of pursuit. A large junction conduit opened up in front of them. McDevitt gave it a 180 check. 'This is the centre line. If we head in this direction, we should make the docking port.'

Directionally challenged, Opi had no option but to agree. Even though she did study the station's schematics, she relied on her handheld to give her directions. At least here they could walk along companion ways that had safety rails. If only their luck would hold out until they got the ship out. Yet, she realised it was registered in McDevitt's name. Lucky, she had her handheld and Alwin glued to her signal at the other end.

McDevitt found an exit and together they walked toward the docking port, joining the other people who were going about their business. Then they turned the corner to where the *Matilda 2* was docked and they had a small welcoming party.

McDevitt grabbed her and placed her up against the wall. He made like they were making out, but instead he was whispering in her ear. 'Did you bring another weapon? This one is empty.'

Opi flicked her gaze up and stared into his. 'Just a little laser pen that someone showed me once.'

He nibbled on the top of her ear. 'Can you give it to me?'

'It's in my boot.'

The welcoming party were taking an interest in them. She remembered then that McDevitt had no shoes. He ran his hand down her butt, along her thigh and then ducked to pluck the laser from her boot. 'Run,' he said.

Opi ran toward the group of men, screaming in alarm. 'He's armed!'

They ran forward and left Opi to open the door to the space dock. The *Matilda 2* looked nice and bright and shiny. Lucky, as purchaser her ID was in the ship's memory and she palmed the lock.

McDevitt was close behind her. He locked the door to the corridor, a weapon propped against his shoulder. He'd stolen one of the guard's laser rifles. Opi didn't want to know what he did to the security team but at least he wasn't too hurt. He had a lump on his cheekbone and a cut on his eyebrow. Someone had got a fist in.

'Fire her up,' McDevitt yelled at her as he secured the lock on the ship.

'You fire it up.' Opi had her handheld out and was frantically keying Alwin. There was a time lag, but still it was better than nothing. If they were held, he'd get them out eventually.

McDevitt swore roundly and went into the control room. He started the launch checklists. Opi joined him, still with her handheld. 'Launch control says green.'

This was a surprise. Different systems maybe or were Burr's goons not stationed in command and control.

The docking bays opened. Opi gaped. They were going to make it. 'Emergency launch procedures. Buckle up.' McDevitt was already strapping himself in. Opi stowed her handheld and did up her safety harness. With a sickening lurch, they were outside the station and shooting for the jumpgate.

Opi sat there speechless. She had done it. She had rescued Owain McDevitt. She checked her calendar. And she'd be back on Earth in time for Burr's campaign launch party. No problem.

Chapter Seventeen

Battle Lines

Once they were sure they were away, McDevitt went into the main cabin to shower and change. Opi sat looking out the viewport at the swirling blur of stars. The trip through the gate should take another twelve hours. One by one, her muscles relaxed and she closed her eyes and let her breathing slow. It was almost done.

The smell of coffee lured her out into the lounge area that served double as the mess. She took the coffee tube McDevitt handed her and sprawled on one of the lounges. 'Thank you,' he said, rather stiffly. 'I appreciate your concern for my welfare.' He was dressed in his Earth Security uniform and he looked divine.

She sat up and put the coffee tube on the side table. 'Why do I get the feeling you're miffed with me?'

He straightened. 'I'm not miffed.'

'Well, then, that's nice to know.'

'You weren't there when I woke up.'

Opi frowned. He meant on Islay 2. 'I had things I needed to do.'

'What's changed then? How come you could spare this little side trip? On your own, too, you crazy woman.'

Opi gritted her teeth. 'I had Alwin mind the fort for me. I needed to make sure Senator Burr didn't know I was gone. After the battle, things were in confusion. I stayed until I knew you were improving. You even talked to me.'

His eyebrow lifted and he leant back a little. 'You did?'

'Yes, of course, I did. I wasn't about to leave Lucinda alone to cope. I stayed as long as I could.'

'I don't remember.'

Opi picked up her handheld. 'Figures.'

'You like throwing your corporate weight around don't you?'

She narrowed her eyelids. 'What do you mean?'

'You buying ships and sending them as gifts. Hobnobbing with politicians and criminals...'

'And potato farmers. You forgot the potatoes.'

Puffed up and menacing, McDevitt approached, plucked the handheld out of her hands and placed it on the side table. She glanced up, saw something in that look, a glint in his blue eyes that warmed her. Not something she was expecting either. The look or her reaction.

He took both her hands and pulled her out of her seat. 'What?'

Then he leant down and tossed her over his shoulder. 'What are you doing?' she asked again, dangling along his back.

'We need to talk.'

'We are talking,' she replied as he headed into his cabin.

'I mean really talk,' he said, and tossed her onto the bed. 'I like the outfit by the way.'

Opi looked down at her black, clinging leather suit. 'Yes, well, it will be difficult to take off.'

McDevitt grinned. 'I can help with that.'

***

Later snuggled in McDevitt's warm embrace, Opi brought him up to speed. 'You had no business taking Lucinda out.'

'I was trying to help. Burr made threats.'

'And taking her shopping to a mall is going to prevent that?'

'I put some security on her after. We went to the mall and there was an attack. Seemingly just a gang, but they didn't behave like a gang. They came straight for us. Security was conveniently absent. Police turned up after we left.'

'How did you deal with this? Did you have security?'

'Yes. But I am the only one licensed for a weapon. I had to stun them. They had, believe it or not, an illegal projectile weapon.'

'Damn it, Opi. Can't you stay out of trouble?'

'I took your daughter shopping. I wasn't trying to get into trouble.'

'You poked Burr though didn't you?'

'A little. I thought he had you. I didn't know where you were.'

'That's no excuse.'

Opi tried pushing him off her. 'It was a public place and I had security.'

He let her up. 'She's fine by the way,' she snapped at him sideways.

He ran his fingers through his hair. They had such a good time, Opi was sad and annoyed that the situation was now all prickly and uncomfortable. She rolled over to get out of bed, but he grabbed her first and rolled on top of her. 'You Ms Gayens have a soft spot for my daughter.'

Opi tried not looking at him, but avoiding his gaze made her eyes ache. 'She is technically my daughter, too, genetically speaking.'

His eyebrows raised. 'Is that all? No tender spot for me in there somewhere?'

'Not at the moment, no. Now if you don't mind I think I'll shower and get ready for landing.'

He inclined his head and helped her out of the bed.

By the time they'd landed, they were back to being cool, professional and distant.

Walking out into the space port on Earth, McDevitt said, 'I have to report in. Are you really going to Burr's campaign launch?'

'Yes, why?'

'You don't have to, you know. We will get the information eventually. There are a lot of interrogations in progress, a lot of information to assess and analyse.'

'I know that, but I have a few strategies up my sleeve.'

His eyes rolled up and he shook his head. 'Please, Opi...Ms Gayens.'

'You think this is funny. That I'm a light weight?'

He shook his head turned her so they faced one another. 'You're not a light weight. I don't want you to get hurt—'

'But?'

'If Burr could be made to slip up, confess, do something outrageous then we could put an end to this a lot quicker.'

'Is this you or Earth Security speaking now.'

His mouth tightened. 'I don't want you anywhere near Burr. I don't own you. I don't control you. Would never try to in any case. But yeah, Earth Security, they don't care about people that much.' He brushed the hair out of her face. 'Not the way I do.'

Opi's heart softened and a small smile escaped. 'Then be ready because this is going to be one hell of a party.'

***

The tinkling of champagne glasses and the hubbub of voices greeted Opi when she exited the lift to the top floor of the Alverston Building. The

Promenade Restaurant took up the whole floor and it was currently crowded with Burr's campaign supporters. An usher walked up to her and smiled when she flashed her VIP invitation card display on her handheld.

'Senator Burr requested that you be brought to him when you arrive. If you'll just follow me.'

Tucking her handheld into its pouch, Opi moved, the split in her long, emerald-green dress revealing her very expensive stockings, the kind that stay up and stay there until you tell them otherwise. It was a pity she had sold the company that made them, but that was life. It didn't mean she had to give up on their brand of Smartwear. Since being bedded by McDevitt, Opi had a new appreciation for her curves and now owned them. Her dress hugged her in a way that no pantsuit dared. Even her walk accentuated the curve of her butt. Opi tried not to grin like a goon. If you've got it flaunt it.

Clages, the host, inclined his head as she passed and continued talking to the two men he was standing with.

The usher cleared the way for her. Opi waved to acquaintances and mouthed hellos to others, even threw a few kisses. It was a campaign launch after all and just about everyone in the business and political world was there, be they friend or foe. A few of them openly gaped at her as she passed them by.

With a light touch, she checked her hair. Normally, she wore it straight but this time, for some unknown reason that had probably a lot to do with McDevitt, she wore it up. Attached to her head was an amazing headpiece that looked like it had been plucked from a garden, an array of silk leaves and bright red flowers. It was quite a likable piece of headwear, purchased on a whim. It made her feel elegant.

From the looks she was receiving, it was having the desired effect. She frowned, wondering exactly what the desired effect was. That she wasn't so old that she couldn't dress up or look good? She grinned. That had been part of it. What else had made her be so bold? Drugs? She nearly laughed out loud. It was, she thought, to exercise herself, to discover who she might be, without all the preprogramed stuff. High-powered corporate exec no longer. It was a mark of her daring to be different, to experiment. Tonight was going to be a big moment.

The crowd parted and at the end of the room, right near a low slung stage was Senator Burr and Madelyn his wife. Their smiles were so large and bright, they might have warranties attached to them. Money back guaranteed to coax or a least cajole money out of their targets.

'Opeia, how lovely to see you,' Madelyn said with a gush and air kissed both cheeks.

Opi gestured with an arm to the crowd. 'And you. I see you have a great turnout. Well done.'

Madelyn pressed her hand to hers and squeezed. 'You are always so delightful.' She leant back to take in Opeia's dress and hairpiece. 'I must say this new you is quite alarming. You are going to steal all the men.'

Senator Burr turned to her. 'So pleased you could make it. I thought you might have been delayed.' He took her hand and squeezed it. Opi grimaced; his grip was hard. He knew about McDevitt, she was sure.

'I would never miss this night,' she said with false enthusiasm. 'I've been keeping my schedule under control so that I could be free for it.'

He cocked his head at her, eyes assessing. 'I was expecting you earlier. The press were doing an interview.'

With a hand to her hair, she smiled. 'Sorry, I was getting my hair done.' She blinked her eyelashes, hoping to dazzle him into thinking she was some airhead from his entourage. Unfortunately, the gesture fell flat. 'Have you got something in your eye? You best get it seen to quickly. We are going to start the formal part soon. Here,' he pushed a glass of pink champagne into her hands. 'Smile.'

There was a media bot and Opeia lifted her glass to it. Opeia shook her head, wishing herself miles away. Then again, maybe she didn't wish herself that far away. It was going to be an interesting night after all.

A tray of canapes passed her by. Opi snagged one, some sort of shrimp roll. It was tasty. As she'd forgotten to eat in the lead up to this gig, she was feeling the champagne rather too much for this early into the proceedings.

Another tray swept passed and she grabbed two of the portions. These seemed to be a mushroom tart. They went down and she followed up with a sip from her glass.

The PA system engaged. Senator Burr started his speech. He spoke about his record on law and order, his support for the poor and the disenfranchised. All total crap as far as Opi was concerned.

A number of key supporters got up. Business and religious leaders, putting their support behind Burr's campaign.

'Now this evening, we have a special guest. One of the most illustrious business leaders of our time. I should say the most illustrious for she has a hand in every pie. Just about everything you wear or eat or have in your house has passed through one of her subsidiaries.

'I've known this woman for a long time, I've seen her grow and mature into the wonderful person she is today. She is incredibly smart, loyal and courageous. Most recently, she was lauded in the press for her part in breaking up the apparatus that supported those vicious criminals, the space pirates. I give you my good friend, Ms Opeia Gayens, Head of AllEarth Corp.'

The applause was almost deafening. Opi's knees trembled and she wished herself elsewhere. For a moment, she thought she was going to falter, that she wasn't going to go through with it. Yet, she had to do this. It would have been better if McDevitt had come through with some conclusive evidence. It would have been so much easier. Perhaps, Burr wouldn't have gone through with his launch if charges were already pending.

Closing her eyes for a moment to gather her resolve, she could be grateful that McDevitt was not being held hostage by Burr, nor the prisoners either. Lucinda was in her father's safe hands. It was between Opi and the senator. She could do this.

Taking a step, Burr took her hand to lead her to the podium. He squeezed her hand sharply and she smiled, beaming out to him and to his audience.

'Thank you for those kind words, Senator Burr. Good evening ladies, gentlemen and others and welcome to the launch of Senator Burr's campaign. You have already had a number of prominent people pledge their support to the Burr campaign.' Her gaze flicked to Burr. He smiled and acknowledged her words by nodding. 'They have stood before you and regaled you with his achievements, his strengths and his plans for the future of our government. I regret to say that I will not be pledging my support for Senator Burr.' A collective gasp greeted words.

Before Senator Burr could stop her she went on, even as a staffer was reaching for the microphone. 'I cannot in all conscience stand before you and lie—'

As Burr himself hadn't tackled her from the stage, she went on, dodging the staffer who was making cut throat motions to the techs. 'I find that I cannot agree with Senator Burr's approach to law and order or the way he conducts himself—'

A bull roar exploded from the sidelines. 'You bitch,' Burr screeched as he dove for her, hands aiming for her neck.

As his hands gripped her throat, she fell back, still gripping the mic. 'I'll kill you for this!' he hissed in her ear and his voice was broadcast over the PA system. Opi was finding it hard to breathe. Her head piece was wrenched off her scalp.

'I'll destroy you, your family and everyone you care about.' He loomed above her, spittle flying.

Opi pulled at his hands and sucked in a desperate breath. He was squeezing her throat. She tried to kick him, but her legs were trapped by her long dress.

Hands grabbed at the Senator, lifting him away. Opi choked and gasped as her airways were freed. Sitting there hunched over trying to speak, she couldn't get a word out. The crowd had gone crazy. People crying, screaming, running about. Burr looked around him, straightened his suit with a tug and motioned to his security team. 'Get her off the stage.' Then he tagged a staffer. 'Get them to play some music. Loud!'

'Yessir!'

Before she could blink, she'd been tackled to the floor again and dragged from the room. Her dress tore and her stay ups came down despite instructions otherwise.

In an anteroom, she was plonked in a chair. Burr came in like a bull to a red cape and slapped her across the face. 'How dare you? You'll pay for this insult.'

Opi tongued the side of her mouth. The slap had smashed her teeth into the soft flesh. 'You have such good manners Burr. It amazes me why your acquaintances don't talk about them more.'

His security team stood around her, dominating with their size and their side arms. 'You have lost your mind.'

She grinned. 'I'm quite lucid. I don't take well to threats.'

'What threats? You're making that up. You said you'd support me while you were head of AllEarth Corp.'

'That was true. I did.'

'So what gives?'

'It's a little premature to elaborate—'

The blow rocked her head back. The world span. Her mouth and throat filled with blood and she coughed it back up. She was too stunned to respond or protect herself.

Just then, loud banging buckled the door. Yells, cries and a scream. More bodies in the room. Her chair rocked, and nearly overbalanced as someone blundered into it.

'Senator Burr! Step away from Ms Gayens.' That sounded like McDevitt's voice.

'Who the hell are you? Shit! Earth security—'

'Don't go anywhere, senator. As well as for assault, attempted murder, you are under arrest for corruption, conspiracy and interstellar piracy.'

From what Opi could understand they had done it. She laughed and spat blood. Her eyesight was affected. The room span. It was the blow and the champagne.

Burr screamed protests as he was dragged away. 'You will never be safe, McDevitt. I'll come for you. My people with come for you.'

She smiled stupidly. Got him.

'Get a doctor in here, quickly.' McDevitt shouted.

'Shh shh. Not too loud.' Opi managed to get out. She lifted a hand but McDevitt grabbed it and squeezed.

'Don't touch it. I think your nose is broken. Opi I'm so sorry. We had to fight our way in here.'

'It was bound to happen. He was never going to take it well. I couldn't support him, Owain. I just couldn't even though I didn't have any evidence to prove my case. I just knew he was behind it.'

'I know. Shh... I know. We have the evidence now. He'll go down believe me. We not only got him but all his little co-conspirators.'

Her vision was clearing. 'You don't have your uniform on. It looked so pretty.'

McDevitt looked like he was smiling. She couldn't tell, he had two mouths.

'Did it?'

'Oh yes...' she frowned. 'Thank you for coming.'

He leant forward. 'Sorry, I wasn't faster. I tried to protect you.'

Opi sat back and swallowed a large blood clot that glugged in the back of her throat and pulled a face. 'Yuck.' Then she remembered what she was saying. 'Protect me? I was protecting you!'

He grinned at her. 'Here's the doctor. Now be good.'

'Don't leave me,' she said in her best pitiful voice. Her eyebrows rose and then she grimaced. It hurt to move her face. 'He punched me in the face. Damn it. That's not right.'

'Don't worry. By the way he fought off security when they pulled him out of here, I think he'll have a much worse blood nose than you.'

'Hello, Ms Gayens. I'm Doctor Traynor. Now let's have a look at you.' The doctor told her to look at him, follow his fingers. She tried but it was a blur. She peered into his face. 'McDevitt is much prettier than you.'

'I see,' Doctor Traynor said. 'I believe Ms Gayens is concussed and that looks like a broken nose. We should take her to hospital. There's not much I can do here but give her some pain relief.'

'Do it,' McDevitt said. 'We'll get her transported. Just make her comfortable.' A large strong hand gripped hers. 'Opi, it's me, Owain. I'll stay with you, okay?'

'Stay with me. I don't want to be alone.'

A sting on her upper arm and the chaos surrounding her faded from view.

McDevitt said in her ear. 'Relax. I'll be with you all the way.'

Chapter Eighteen

It's a Wrap

Opi was alone when she woke up in her hospital room. At first she was worried. Hadn't McDevitt been there? Hadn't he rescued her from Burr?

The ache in her head and face let her know that she hadn't imagined that scene. She had caused an almost riot. Burr had lost it and Earth Security had taken him away. Her recollection wasn't too clear. She distinctly remembered saying some stupid, frivolous things to McDevitt. Cringing, she looked around the room, if just to stop remembering what her mouth had said when it was detached from her brain.

From her comms unit, she saw that it was three days later. She'd been out that long. Wow, that was some concussion.

The sound of a switch and someone moving about alerted her that she wasn't alone after all. A nurse hovered. 'Where's McDevitt?'

The nurse checked her vitals on the monitor above the bed. 'You mean the tall gentleman who has been sitting by your bed for days?'

Opi scanned the room. There was a chair pulled up near the bed. No other signs that someone had been there. 'Yes, I suppose so.' She fingered the bandage on her face. Her whole face was numb and she could taste blood in the back of her throat.

'He's a handsome man. Very attentive,' the nurse said.

Opi tried to clear her throat and found it obstructed. She sat up suddenly and the room span. She was still woozy. She tried to swallow but found that she couldn't. A huge blood clot was descending down the back of her throat. She retched and slapped the bedcovers and pointed. The nurse calmly went to the cabinet and brought over a small basin and held it while Opi hacked and choked. Then desperate for breath, she shoved her fingers into her mouth and groped for the clot. Finally, she got hold of the enormous bloody blob and drew it out of her mouth, retching as she did so. Even after she'd cleared her throat, she vomited, but she had nothing in her stomach. Laying there panting and wiping her mouth, she was glad McDevitt hadn't been there to witness that. She'd experienced enough embarrassing moments in his company to last a lifetime. It was a miracle she could stand to be in the same room with him. Whether by accident or design, McDevitt had seen her at her most vulnerable. 'Can I see a mirror?' she asked weakly.

The nurse made a face but extracted one out of the bedside drawer.

Opi nearly dropped it. Her eyes were black and swollen. A bandage covered most of her face. Her hair was stuck up in spikes and looked absolutely filthy. Her mouth had dried blood caked in the corners and her lips were also misshapen with swelling. Her moan escaped before she could stop it.

The nurse smiled at her and held out her hand for the mirror. 'You look much better today.'

Opi just moaned louder and closed her eyes. McDevitt had seen her looking trashed. Totally trashed. The universe had no mercy. Not that she normally cared what other people thought, but he was different. They'd been on a date. A disaster date. They really hadn't had much going for them since then either.

Exhausted, she lay back against her pillows feeling very sorry for herself. There were two bonuses in this situation: Burr was caught and her face was numb. She stared morosely at the nurse.

'Your male friend was called away. He said to tell you he'd try to get back this evening. There have been developments he said.'

She acknowledged this information with a slow nod of her head. Then something the nurse had given her sent her off to sleep again.

When she next woke, Rae and Essa were by her bedside. A quick scan of the room revealed no McDevitt. He said he'd come back. He hadn't.

'Opi you were on the news. Your speech has been replayed over and over.'

Essa sniffed. 'Yes, and the news about Burr's arrest. They are now calling you the AllEarth Corp battle maiden. I mean some people are just silly.'

Opi managed a wan smile. But it hurt so she stopped it. 'When does the bandage come off?'

Rae grinned at her. 'Well the doctor told us in a couple of days. It will be a good as new. You won't snore or anything anymore.'

'I don't snore.'

Rae and Essa shared a look and laughed. 'Sure you don't. But you must admit you do drool.'

'I don't drool either. Stop disrespecting your mother. I'm injured.'

Rae leant in and pointed to the pillow. 'Is that a drool mark?'

'Stop. You're making me laugh and it hurts.'

'Don't worry it will be better soon,' Rae said and hugged her. Essa dropped a kiss on her forehead.

'We better go, mother. That dragon of a nurse said we could only have fifteen minutes and you slept for ten of those.'

They squeezed her hand and left.

The next morning she woke and up and there was still no sign of McDevitt. What a pain that he had hung around for three days and then left. Then she remembered what she had done. How bitter he had been over her not being there. Was he paying her back?

The bandages came off. Her nose was still tender but the swelling had come right down. 'Take it easy for a day or two and it will be fine. Any headaches?'

Opi wanted to respond that her life ached, but shook her head slowly. She felt like crap but as she wanted to go home there was no point in informing the doctor of that fact.

***

The security guard nodded from his place by the gate and she walked up the path and let herself into her house. Her bed looked inviting so she climbed into it, making sure she didn't sleep on her face. She didn't want a lopsided nose. Her dreams were full of McDevitt, various explorations of why he didn't come back to see her. Why he hadn't called. All were negative. She was better off not even thinking of him.

The next day she went into her office. After dealing with her backlog of correspondence her comms unit chimed. It was McDevitt. She took a big breath and readied herself.

'Hello McDevitt. What can I do for you?'

'Hi Opi. Sorry I didn't make it back to the hospital. I went there and they said you'd gone home. The nose is looking good.'

'It's functional. What can I do for you? I'm pretty busy.'

'Oh? Right. Well I just wanted to let you know that Burr is going down. He's confessed and is trying to plea bargain.'

'Figures. You did a good job. I'm sure you'll get a promotion.'

'I don't want one. I'm hoping it's enough to let me off the hook. Then I'll head back to Islay 2.'

'Oh right, your potatoes. Well, best of luck with that.' She looked at her email, pretended that it was something else. 'Look, I've got to go. I've got meetings back to back. Give my love to Lucinda and have a safe trip back home.'

There was a pause. Opi couldn't look at him. 'Right. I'll be seeing you around then.'

She threw him a fake smile. 'Yes. Sure. One day. When our schedules coincide.'

He keyed off. Opi put her head down on her desk and cried like her heart was breaking. It was breaking. Why had she done that? Why had she pushed him away? It was too complicated to work out. Caring for someone exposed you to hurt. She couldn't do that, couldn't go there.

Dayton called her. 'Time to make the decision. I can't hold off any longer.'

'Do it!'

One more night as head of AllEarth Corp. One more night as the richest woman on Earth and elsewhere. She'd done what she had set out to do. She had ended the space pirates. Now, she had to get free of her own shackles. Her daughters didn't want their inheritance. She admired them for that. She hadn't been so brave in her own choices.

Yet, if her daughters could choose their own lives. Why couldn't she? At first she was just going to downsize, try and live a little more. Then she extended her plans and looked hard at the business and what she wanted and what she needed. There was too much wealth for one person to enjoy.

The way she led her life made her realise that she didn't enjoy it. There were threats to her person, threats of kidnap, death. There were all her responsibilities. The risk to her family. Being so rich meant she could do a lot of things the ordinary person couldn't, but it also meant that she had little of the freedom that the ordinary person enjoyed. So she'd thought up a plan. One where no one suffers.

The businesses continue but broken up and owned in part by a staff fund. A lot of the money she'd hived off to charities, and built up a huge trust fund for her philanthropic interests, clones and development issues for the poor. There was plenty of money to see her through her life and probably the next.

Dayton put through the last of the share transactions, sent through the notices to the stock exchange, then after they had processed it and made an announcement to the trading floor and submitted the press releases.

Opi paced up and down all morning. It wasn't long before her comms unit went haywire. She disconnected it. Not long after that the sounds of a commotion reached her. Taking a peep out the window, she saw the gathering crowd. The hum of a media bot alerted her to its approach and she twitched the blind closed.

With a satisfied smile, she hit the privacy screen and the bot sped away before its circuits overloaded. The crowd at her gate grew even bigger by the evening. Just as well she had no meetings to go to.

When it got too much for her, she sent off a pre-recorded message to the press and on general broadcast. She called it her long good bye, outlining the changes she had made, the new ownership arrangements and her request for privacy.

***

Opi sat on the beach, her feet buried in the warm, soft sand. Little waves swam up to tease her toes. The horizon was fuzzy with light and pollution. The tide was going out, fading away and she could see the ruins of the town that once stood on the coast emerge from its watery grave. With rising seas humans had to adapt.

The afternoon sun winked on the tufts of water, making the foam flecks glitter over the darker blue sea beneath. Her mind was busy. She didn't want it to be so. After so much anxiety, so much decision, her mind should be empty. Yet the habit of worry still clung to her. It was a skin too often worn to be discarded. She climbed to her feet, letting the cool water caress them, cool them. Learning to unwind hadn't been part of her life lesson. Of course, her celebrity status was still going to haunt her. Curiosity about the woman who walked away from her trillions, her high flying career, that wasn't going to fade very quickly.

Ever since Masher had tortured her, threatened Rae and they'd been rescued by Essa, she'd been planning for this time. Now she was on the beach, nothing left to do.

It was time to find out who Opeia was, who Opi was. She chuckled to herself. Looking back, she could see it had been coming on for a while, even before she started the process of disentangling herself from that life. Power had seemed a good thing. Yet, powerlessness had taught her that it was nothing. Powerlessness had taught her that life, and what you do with it, is important.

Seagulls cawing made her look up and around. The glistening wet sand, high, distant clouds and the beach house. Something she'd bought and was going to keep. The nearby village was called Seahaven and that is what it was to her—a haven.

A cooling breeze brought gooseflesh out on her arms and she rubbed at her skin and made for the house. It was empty.

Inside she drew the rug that decorated the lounge over her shoulders and stepped barefoot into the kitchen. The sun draped itself in robes of orange and peach and yellow. A perfect setting for some wine.

As she sat on the porch, foot resting on a stool and sipped Sauvignon Blanc, she said goodbye to the last days of her old life and the welcomed the new. It was hard just to sit there, not to think or do something. In this she gained new insights about herself.

As the weeks passed, Opi grew accustomed to her new life. Rae and Essa had welcomed the change. Were happy for her. Neither questioned it. That acceptance meant the world to her. Sometimes, she thought about a retro red dress and a dinner date. The bizarre events that followed. With some regret, she remembered that smile and the blue of McDevitt's eyes. It could never be. When it came down to it, she couldn't fall in love with her clone's widower.

***

Coming back from a meeting with the board her OREL Foundation, Opi kicked off her heels and sighed gratefully and then went for a walk along the beach. She grinned at the name, it stood for Opeia, Rae, Essa and Lucinda. Perfect.

On her return, she lowered herself to the decking and sat there with her bare feet dangling, looking out of the sea. She wrestled with indecision. The thought of visiting Islay 2 had crossed her mind more than once. Often she dreamed of Lucinda, of that picnic and the horses, of the bright day and the clean air. Of lying on a blanket with Owain's arms around her. All new and strange experiences, ones that had left a mark on her. But she had no rights there. That life belonged to her clone, Belle. McDevitt was in love with his wife. Not Opi.

Opi was the echo, the hollow replacement that faded into nothing.

When her mind strayed to that night in McDevitt's bed, her hands clenched and she became restless. *Damn. Damn. Damn.* Why did she have to remember that? The soft brush of his fingertips on her cheek, the heat of him enclosing her...

'When were you going to tell me?' A familiar voice spoke to her from the sand below.

Opi blinked, and shook her head. No longer dreams but auditory illusions.

'Opi? Won't you even look at me?'

She turned her head slowly and there he was. He was wearing civilian clothes. His hair was longer than its previous military cut. He looked relaxed, healthier, in is casual trousers and t-shirt. Not as spiffy as his uniform but he looked good, less haggard.

'McDevitt?'

He nodded, his gaze wary. 'You could, at least, after all we have been through call me Owain.'

'Owain, what are you doing here? I thought you'd gone back to Islay 2.'

'I did go there after we last spoke. However, it has come to my attention that you left out a few details about your life, your future in that conversation we had. Why didn't you tell me?'

Opi bit her lip. This was true. 'I couldn't tell anyone and until I actually did it wasn't sure I would or could. There are strict rules of disclosure with the stock exchange.'

'Not even that you were thinking about it?'

'Mmm like I said I hadn't committed. Not fully. Besides I didn't think we were on such terms.'

'Terms? You mean you didn't want me around? Is that it?'

Opi frowned. 'That's not what I said actually. But you weren't around if you recall. You said you would be but you weren't.'

'And that upset you didn't it? I was there for days. Then I was recalled to duty. I had to leave. So that's why you wouldn't give me the time of day. You gave me the brush off. That's all you could spare. You didn't give me a hint.'

'A hint? What hint?'

'That some old rancher like me could have a chance with you?'

'Some old rancher?' What was he talking about? 'Oh, you mean you?'

'Yes, me. Who else is there?'

'I hadn't really given it any thought.'

'Oh now you're just being insulting. Are you going to invite me in or are you just going to hurl insults at me from there?'

'Oh...sure come on up. I don't have much in...I wasn't expecting guests. There is probably only wine and cheese.'

He climbed up on the deck, put his hand out to her. She took it and he helped her up to her feet. Her eyes travelled over him, her mind putting the details in order, reviving her memory of him down in her senses, in her emotions. Her body, her hormones, her heart responded with such clamouring force she could hardly speak.

'Shall we?' He said, opening up his arm to indicate the door.

'Y...yes.'

She was bare. Stripped. There was no company to hide behind. No demand on her time. It was just her and him. Her heart thudded. This could not be happening. How had he got around the security? There, already she was looking for props, for excuses because she couldn't bear to admit that she craved, she desired, she wanted with all her heart and body and mind.

Unable to function, she stood there stupidly. He glanced at her, grinned and went to the fridge. 'Sit,' he said and then handed her a glass of wine.

The glass touched her lips. Lips he had kissed. She had to stop thinking about that.

'Nice place you have here.'

'Yes, it is. Quiet...' She couldn't think of anything else to say. She avoided looking at him, casting her gaze about the room, looking at nothing in particular.

'So, you couldn't tell me about AllEarth Corp and your quitting and divestment and so on before you did it. Why the hell didn't you tell me after you did?'

'It's complicated.'

He blinked. 'Complicated?'

He gestured to the simple house she'd been hiding out in for the best part of two months. 'What's complicated about this? Don't you know what you want?'

The wine spilled down her hands as she jerked when he spoke. Her panicked gaze met his. 'How did you know that?'

'I don't know it. But I feared it.'

'Feared it? Why?'

'Because I love you, Opi. I want to share my life with you. Yet I understand there are complications for you because of Belle.'

'Yes. That's kinda weird.'

He shrugged. 'You look like her. I can't change that. You can't change that. But you are not her. Not in the least. Your mannerisms are different. What you did with your life is different. When I look at you I don't see her. I see Opi and possibilities open up inside me. I didn't think I'd find someone I'd want to share my life on Islay 2. I wasn't even looking. Then you touched my life with kindness. Just that light touch enchanted me and then we met. It was the craziest time of my life. We both nearly lost our lives. We fought. We loved. Now we need to see if we can move beyond that.

'When you didn't come to me on Islay 2, I admit I was hurt. Deeply hurt. I thought all kinds of things. Angry things. Hurt things. Then I started thinking about how it must be for you. What a huge transition it must be going from head of AllEarth Corp, to dismantling the conglomerate that it was, giving away all that money and to being just you. I realised that I couldn't have done that. Not only don't I have the brains, I don't have the nerve and the sheer goddam courage.

'You beat the bloody space pirates. They are gutted. Gone. I know because I checked. It was my job. You snatched that job out of my hands and you rammed those bastards into the next century.'

'But... I couldn't have done it without you. In that battle in space I'd have been killed. Your piloting saved us both.'

'You didn't want my help.'

'I know, but I welcomed it. When I understood. You were trying to save me. I wanted to save you.'

His forehead crinkled. 'So you cared about me?'

'Yes, I cared. I do care still.'

Owain sculled his wine. 'In that case,' he slid off his chair and came to kneel by hers. He took her glass and put it on the table. 'Opeia would you let this pain in the ass fellow be your husband? Would you consider living on Islay 2 with me, making your life there?'

Opeia's heart beat so hard she could hardly hear. This was a chance for happiness, her happiness. Owain's too. Giving up her corporation had seemed easier than this. Owain cupped her chin, his blue eyes staring into hers. 'Opi?'

He brushed his lips against her mouth. The contact shocked her. It was like a circuit closed and the electricity leaped. Her mouth sought his, closed hungrily. Arms around his neck, she held him close. He returned her kiss in kind. With her body pressed close to his, she found that lust she had for him rekindled. All her worries and fears fell away. She could do this. She could. She would.

Opi leant back, breaking the kiss. Owain's eyes smouldered, but his lips wet from her kiss had a smile playing on them. 'Is that a yes?'

'Yes,' she said. Tears welled up in her eyes. Damn the bloody things. They cramped her style.

'I like the way you say yes. Can you say it again?'

Opi just grabbed him to her and devoured his mouth, leaving him gasping. 'That was definitely a serious yes.'

Opi laughed.

'So would that yes mean that you want me to stay the night, warm your bed?'

She kissed him again, running her fingers through his short hair, not able to grab any and give it a good tug.

'Oh, definitely I like this new style of communication. You should live in lonely cottages more often.'

Opi giggled and sniffed. So she was happy and emotional. This was, of course, a big moment in her life. A smile lit her face. It was the first day of the rest of her life.

A squeal escaped as he swooped and drew her into his arms. 'Which way?'

Her bedroom was on the main floor so she pointed. 'But we have no food.'

'You hungry? I've ordered dinner to be delivered in two hours. I think that's enough time to work on our appetites.'

He kissed her surprised mouth and kicked open the door. 'Nice. You were expecting me I think.'

She looked down at the bed and shook her head. Then he tossed her onto the mattress. 'Oh?'

Before she had time to protest, Owain was covering her with his body. 'It's big enough for both of us.' Then he nuzzled her neck. The sensation of his soft lips on her vulnerable neck took her back to Islay 2, to that night of passion. A night she never thought she'd have. But did and couldn't forget.

Was it wrong to want more? To want him, his heat and his muscle sliding against her.

Their mouths duelled, then consumed. Opi was lost in his kiss, so lost she didn't even notice when he made short work of her clothes. Then to even the score she dispensed with his. He slapped her lightly on the rump.

'I love your beautiful ass.'

Opi smiled. She thought he did have an affection for her butt, he'd had plenty of opportunity to get used to seeing it.

He cupped her breasts. 'These are a delight. All of you is a feast for the eyes. And that soft heart of yours and that amazing head for business. They do things to me. Things I didn't think were possible. They make my heart thud, you make it thud. Put your hand here and see for yourself.'

She did, his heart was beating fast. So was hers. She ran a finger along his chin. 'I like your face.'

He kissed the palm of her hand. 'I like all of you, Opi. I think I've loved you from when you told me to stop looking at your ass.'

Opi burst out laughing, rolled around the bed laughing. Owain just grinned like a loon. 'You know you've totally broken the mood here.'

Opi laughed some more. 'It was your fault. You mentioned that horrible date and the dress and my butt and you eyeing it off.'

'I couldn't help it. The thing was there in front of me, blocking my escape.'

The laughter welled up again and then she quieted, keeping her dark eyes pinned to Owain and then the mood shifted and he was there, pulling her back into his arms, kissing her soundly and then they were touching again.

'I know you're scared, Opi,' he said as he held her. 'I can imagine it has been an amazing transition for you. But on Islay 2 there is scope there for you to find yourself. I want you there with me, but if it really doesn't work for you then I won't keep you there. I only want you with me because you want it. Because you love me.'

'I know,' she said softly, almost whispering. 'You're a fair man. I won't mess with you. The future does scare me. Not because of insecurity about who I am or what I feel for you. It's because it's so free. There is no map there anymore. My life is free for me to choose. It's like stepping out of an airlock without a tether. I'm not sure where I'll end up.'

He held her to him, rubbed firm hands along her back. Opi lay against his body, enjoying the firmness of him. 'I can understand your fear. It's what most people face every day. You were in a mould. You conformed. Did your best and did a great job of it. Now you're free to choose.'

They leant their foreheads together. 'I chose freedom,' she said studying his face, wanting to imbed the image of it in her mind forever, wanting to hold this moment close and still. 'Then I chose you.'

'I chose you too. I guess that makes it a deal.'

'Sounds like one to me. Not a standard contract though.'

'What do you mean?'

'Well there's offer and acceptance, but what about fulfilling the contract, paying for services offered and accepted?'

He let out a bark of laughter. 'You capitalist! What am I? The contract or the payment?'

Opi considered this for a moment. 'I think it will be ongoing but right now I think a down payment is in order.'

Later she added, 'I think I have a marketing strategy for your potatoes.'

McDevitt laughed. 'Of course you do.'

***

The wedding took place in the gardens of the McDevitt homestead on Islay 2. Just about every inhabitant of the planet attended. Most of them bought their own food and produce and camped on the newly harvested fields. Rae, Essa and Lucinda looked lovely in their matching bride's maid dresses. Opi couldn't stop smiling when she looked at them.

A few stern words from the girls made her stop with the looking and the sighing and repeating over and over that they were beautiful on the grounds that she was embarrassing them.

Every time Owain did more than peck her on the cheek, all three of them groaned or said 'eeewww'. They were quite happy for their mother to get married, they just didn't like the thought of her having sex.

Opi was sure that Owain got a bit out of hand just so he could scandalise the children. As a former executive of a multisector corporation, she was above such paltry tricks. She just came out straight and told them that Owain was a very good lover, who kept her occupied most of the night, and she wondered how on earth she could keep awake during the ceremony. Then she hid her smile behind her veil as Rae, Essa and Lucinda turned various shades of grey, green and violet as they lurched away to lose their lunches. *Kids!*

The End

If you loved Opi and Battles the Space Pirates then check out the rest of the Love and Space Pirates Series.

Rayessa and the Space Pirates

Sixteen-year-old Rae Stroder lives in a hollow asteroid, a defunct refuelling station, with a brain-damaged adult, Gris, to keep her company. Low on supplies, they've been eking out an existence for years. Everything changes when Alwin Anton, ultra-clean, smart and handsome AllEarth Corp company auditor, arrives to find disarray. Full of suspicion, he interrogates Rae, threatening her with prosecution for theft. He uncovers the fact that she is not Rae Stroder at all, when space pirates attack.

During the attack, Rae is taken prisoner and Alwin Anton escapes in his space ship. The pirate women prepare Rae for sale on the infamous Centauri slave markets. It's all going badly, when she is purchased by a mysterious Ridallian. Meanwhile, the space pirates are out to kill Alwin Anton because he holds the secret to Rae's true identity. It's a race against time to unravel the intrigue of Rae's past to secure her future.

Buy Rayessa and the Space Pirates from Amazon.com

And

Rae and Essa's Space Adventures

Essa Gayens is starting to accept her sister Rae into her life, sharing a dorm room in their swanky private school on Earth. Smarter, savvier and more in touch with the world than Rae, Essa's feelings of superiority and advantage are shaken when their mother goes missing, along with Rae's boyfriend, Alwin.

When Rae takes off after them into outer space, Essa is spurred into action. Very soon, Essa is hot on her trail, sneaking out of school, bribing officials and begging Captain Thorn Hanover to take her on his ship.

Thorn is a hunk, and Essa is thrilled with the prospect of an interesting trip, but Thorn has no interest in a spoiled rich girl. Not only does he reject her advances, he sets her up on the chore roster and expects her to work for her passage.

Essa has never been anything but a pampered princess, but both Rae and Thorn are challenging her to dig deeper, to be more. But to aspire is to risk failure, and Essa has never really risked anything before. Can she start with her heart?

Buy Rae and Essa's Space Adventures from Amazon.com

www.ingramcontent.com/pod-product-compliance
Lightning Source LLC
Chambersburg PA
CBHW050402110726
47899CB00008B/2617